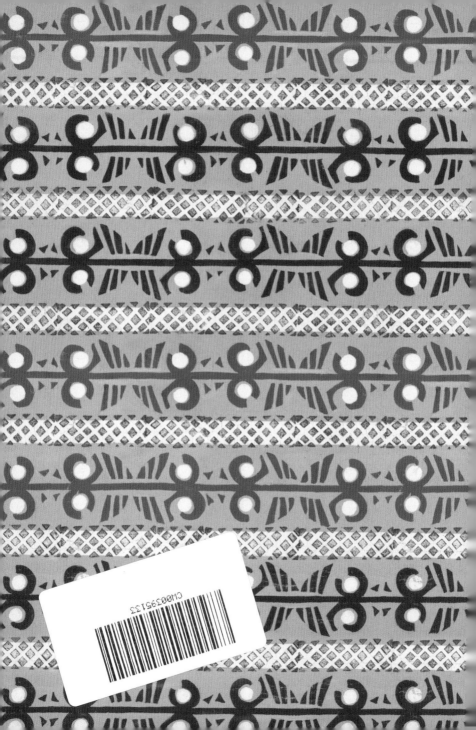

CM0039313

THE WOMAN NOVELIST AND
OTHER STORIES

Persephone Book Nº64
Published by Persephone Books Ltd 2006
reprinted 2015

First published as *Halfway Down the Cliff*
by Editions Poetry London (PL)/
Nicholson and Watson in 1946; except for
'The Woman Novelist', not previously published.

Endpapers taken from an untitled fabric design in
potato prints and paint on sugar paper by
Alma Ramsey-Hosking c. 1942
© Hosking Houses Trust

Typeset in ITC Baskerville by Keystroke,
Jacaranda Lodge, Wolverhampton

Colour by Banbury Litho

Printed and bound in Germany
by GGP Media GmbH, Poessneck

978 1903155 547

Persephone Books Ltd
59 Lamb's Conduit Street
London WC1N 3NB
020 7242 9292

www.persephonebooks.co.uk

THE WOMAN NOVELIST AND
OTHER STORIES

by

DIANA GARDNER

with a preface by

CLAIRE GARDNER

PERSEPHONE BOOKS
LONDON

CONTENTS

PREFACE

In 1977, when she was 64, my aunt Diana Gardner wrote, in a memoir of her early life: 'I had wanted to write short stories from the age of eleven – starting off with a "thriller" – and gradually developing into short character-sequences . . . hinting at the profundities of existence just behind the exterior activity of life. Or at any rate that was what I hoped I was writing, and what for me, was the value, in fact, the quintessential, gemlike quality of the short story as "an art form."'

This was her conception of a short story after she had achieved success. Earlier, in her journal of 1931 – when she was only 18 and had not yet published anything – she describes the places she visits (a park in Amersham, a country church in Hughenden, a furniture shop in Bedford and so on) almost as backdrops for a story. And there are numerous jottings of a few lines called 'idea for a story'.

It was in this period (and earlier) that she cared for her father almost single-handedly. He had a form of nervous exhaustion brought on by the early death of my grandmother (when Diana was 9), followed by the death of his own mother. He refused to see his sons for some time and only wanted to

be looked after by his daughter. In the mid-1930s, a friend of the family persuaded him to allow Diana to go to art school so that she could have a life of her own. By this time he had recovered and the relationships with his sons (my father Paul and Uncle Jock) had been re-established.

Although writing was Diana's favourite form of expression, she was also very interested in art. She attended the Regent Street Polytechnic and the Westminster School of Art, where she was taught by, and became a friend of, Mervyn Peake. All the time she was learning drawing and wood-engraving, however, she continued to write short stories. It was when the Second World War broke out and she had decided to stay in the country, in Rodmell, Sussex, where she and her father had bought a thatched cottage in 1934, that she began to 'work very much harder' at the stories. She notes that she had more time for writing, for instance, during air-raid watching sessions at night – time 'with the quiet darkness outside'.

When, in November, 1940, Diana received her first acceptance of a short story 'The Land Girl' from Cyril Connolly, the editor of the magazine *Horizon*, she was overjoyed. His acceptance postcard is worth quoting. Connolly writes:

> I like your story 'Land Girl' and am putting it in our Christmas number. I am so glad you wrote it and not DH Lawrence, or we should have had such a portentous affair between the man of the soil, with his lore, and the young woman. She sounds delightful.

This is not quite how Diana (or probably the reader) sees the character of the land girl and clearly Connolly was being provocative. She noted:

> There was of course no particular landgirl in mind, only oddly the idea that a short story by HE Bates called, I think, 'The Sisters' and which had recently been published, did not go far enough in analysing and describing the destructive lengths to which a jealous female might go; therefore, according to myself this would be a truer version.

I should add here that some time after purchasing the Thatched Cottage in Rodmell, Diana discovered that Virginia and Leonard Woolf had a house in the same village. Diana was a great admirer of Virginia Woolf's writing and some of the entries in her 1931 journal mentioned above are quotations from *The Waves*, followed by her comments. Diana and my father, being neighbours of the Woolfs, became acquainted with them and went to tea with them on several occasions. Diana also mentioned to me that *Horizon* printed advance leaflets of the contents of their next issue. One of these leaflets, where her name and the title of her story appeared, was brought round to Thatched Cottage by Virginia Woolf's 'help', Louie Everest. Virginia had underlined Diana's story and written in green ink something like 'Congratulations, VW' in the margin.

'The Land Girl' was favourably received and Diana began to be considered a promising young writer. In fact, in

the 1940s her stories appeared in almost every literary magazine of the time and were reviewed in major newspapers. Her short stories were also included in collections such as the *Grey Walls Stories* alongside authors such as Olivia Manning, Henry Miller and Stephen Spender.

Back in 1938, Diana had met the Indian author and editor Tambimuttu (of Tamil origin) when he was putting together the first issue of *Poetry London*. She was struck by his vision of a new type of poetry magazine and his pleasure in all art forms. Three of my aunt's wood engravings were used by Tambi (as friends affectionately called him) to illustrate the first number of *Poetry London*. Interestingly, in his *Memoirs of the Forties* (published in 1965), J. Maclaren-Ross tells a humorous anecdote regarding Tambi, Diana and himself. He recounts that Tambi thought it would be good for his (Maclaren-Ross's) career

> . . . to marry a girl called Diana Gardner, whose excellent collection of short stories *Halfway Down the Cliff* he [Tambi] later published. She too had made a big stir in *Horizon* with 'The Land Girl' and her story 'Crossing the Atlantic' had a harsh impersonal cynicism seldom found in feminine fiction at this period. Tambi felt that as presumably kindred souls we should make it a *Horizon* wedding, with Cyril Connolly to give away the bride and famous contributors outside the church to hold copies of the magazine over us when we emerged.

Maclaren-Ross never actually met Diana and when she came

across this anecdote she was surprised and amused. Tambi had never mentioned his matchmaking plan to her! But when Tambi and my aunt happened to meet in London during the war he would say 'Ah, the land girl' and enthusiastically put his arms right round her. This use of his nickname for her is recounted by Diana in her recollection of Tambi in the book *Tambimuttu: Bridge between Two Worlds* (ed. Jane Williams, 1989).

As Maclaren-Ross mentioned in his anecdote, Tambimuttu published Diana's collection of short stories in his Editions Poetry London (PL) in 1946. I have Diana and Tambimuttu's correspondence – which goes from July 1944 to March 1945 – about this project (which must have already been touched upon during one of their conversations). In his letter of October 1944 he thanks Diana for the collection and expresses his enthusiasm for it. Other letters regard the sequence of stories, number of words and the poor quality of paper during the war years. This present selection includes fourteen of Diana's best stories from the original collection, leaves five out and adds a previously unpublished short story 'The Woman Novelist' which was written in 1950.

Diana as a girl loved horror stories and had started off writing, as has been said, with a 'thriller' (never published and which I have not found in her papers). Her attraction to this genre can be seen in the macabre elements in four of the stories in this collection: 'Miss Carmichael's Bed', 'Crossing the Atlantic', The Couple from London' and 'Mrs Lumley'. However, rather than being the main focus of the stories, the purpose of these elements seems to be that of adding to

the suspense or tension. In a notebook of Diana's called 'My method of writing short stories and novels', written in 1956 and which she thought could be used as notes for a BBC talk (a project she did not pursue), she emphasises the need for tautness and tension in stories:

> A tension of suspense – of the story unfolding . . . the reader never sits down and is utterly content with what is happening at that moment. He is aware always of the impending development which is going to upset – or resolve – that very part which he is at that moment reading about.

Diana's stories are often memorable because of what she calls 'tension' and for their unexpected endings; sometimes these are interesting (almost tragic) anticlimaxes such as in 'No Change', 'Miss Carmichael's Bed' and 'Mrs Lumley'. Some of the stories are set in Germany, which Diana visited in about 1935 for a walking tour with her brother Paul and a mutual friend. Others (including some of those with German settings) are set just before or during the Second World War. Diana was uncertain whether to include some of these ('In the Boathouse', for instance) in the original collection, writing to Tambimuttu in 1944: 'It is a mistake to overdo the war', but in the end they were included. Walter Allen, reviewing Diana's stories in the *Spectator* in 1946, said of 'In the Boathouse': 'She produces by the simplicity, exactness and quietness of her style something very like poetry.' And Fred Urquhart commented in *Tribune* in the same year that '"The Splash" is as good a portrait of a young Nazi as I have read.'

In the same letter to Tambimuttu mentioned above, Diana says of her selection of stories: 'I have included all my genres: satirical sketches, sardonic stories, tragedies, comedies – so that it is representative". To these Persephone Books has added a later story, 'The Woman Novelist', written in 1950, just before Diana began writing her novel *The Indian Woman* (published by Eyre and Spottiswoode in 1954). Although it is a mistake to identify a fictional character with her creator, I am almost sure that the joy in writing expressed by Madeleine, the woman novelist, was similar to that felt by Diana.

My aunt continued writing short stories until about 1962 and several of her non-fiction articles were published in newspapers such as *The Times* and the *Manchester Guardian*, but probably the fact that two more novels, written between 1954–56 and 1957–59, were turned down encouraged her to devote more time to painting. She also felt that there was 'a complete change' in contemporary writing which she did not feel at ease with. She worked as a publicity manager to a publishing firm and then around 1968 took up painting full-time. Her two talents crossed over to a certain extent in her artistic production. In her stories, we can see her painter's eye when she describes the various settings, particularly in her use of colour terms. In 'Summer with the Baron', for instance, when the sun goes down, the water of the lake is 'dark peacock blue', the bathing huts 'warm umber' and the bodies of the bathers 'pinkish brown'. Conversely in her later watercolours – where people and cars appear – every painting seems to tell a story. Writers and painters clearly need a keen sense of observation and Diana certainly had that in abundance.

Although concentrating on watercolour painting in the 1970s and '80s, Diana still wrote: mainly recollections of her early years in Rodmell and of the people she met there and at art school. Two articles on Mervyn Peake and an obituary of his wife Maeve Peake (a friend of hers) were published in *The Mervyn Peake Review*. In the mid-1990s, she felt that her eyesight was not as good as it had been (she was in her eighties) and that painting was going to become more and more difficult. So she began to contemplate writing again and was about to revise her memoirs of Rodmell, the war years and Virginia and Leonard Woolf when she suddenly died at the age of 84 in 1997.

In 1944 a reviewer in *World Review* felt that Diana Gardner, 'nearly always sardonic and unpleasantly near the truth, may well become the Dorothy Parker of our country.' But the comparison does not seem to hold, except perhaps with 'The Land Girl' and 'Crossing the Atlantic'. Walter Allen was surely closer to the truth when he observed that 'Miss Gardner writes very well indeed; her observation is precise, she has a keen eye for colour, and she knows the value of under-statement.' And it was the reviewer in the *Manchester Guardian* who understood Diana Gardner best when he concluded that 'she is without question a gifted artist in a distinctively modern medium in which the poetry and the prose of life, the fantastic, and the factual give spirit and substance to each other.'

Claire Gardner
Turin, 2005

'The House at Hove' was written in October 1941; 'No Change' was written in March 1938 and published in *English Story* in 1941; 'Miss Carmichael's Bed' was written in March 1940 and published in *Life and Letters Today* in May 1942; 'The Land Girl' was written in February 1940 and published in *Horizon* in December 1940; 'Summer Holiday' was written in July 1941 and published in *Phoenix* in Autumn 1946; 'The Woman Novelist' was written in 1950; 'Crossing the Atlantic' was written in November 1940 and published in *Horizon* in September 1942; 'The Couple from London' was written in March 1939; 'Mrs Lumley' was written in August 1943 and published in *The New Saxon Review* in December 1946; 'In the Boathouse' was written in April 1943; 'Halfway down the Cliff' was written in April 1943 and published in *Thirteen Stories* in February 1944; 'The Splash' was written in February 1944 and published in *Rangefinder* in August 1944; 'The Pirate' was written in December 1942 and published in *Writing Today* in October 1943; 'Summer with the Baron' was written in April 1942 and published in February 1943 in *Selected Writing*; 'The Visitation' was written in August 1942 and published in *Life and Letters Today* in October 1942. All the stories except for 'The Woman Novelist' were published in *Halfway Down the Cliff* (1946).

THE WOMAN NOVELIST AND
OTHER STORIES

THE HOUSE AT HOVE

From the upstairs drawing-room of No. 18, the house which my mother took at the beginning of 1920, we could see the white cliffs on the edge of the town and, running towards them, the backs of the driving waves – for the wind was nearly always from the south-west. It was a lovely house, bow-fronted, and faced by two pillars which ran up as high as the cornice below the roof. The terrace in which it was built stood a little higher than the promenade and on grey days the rich ochre of the houses struck a warm note against the cold asphalt of the wide front and the transparent green of the sea.

Although it had been built in the Regency and its rooms were large, it was still easy to run just after the last war. Then servants were plentiful, and because of the growth of the town the rents were not high – although Mother was un-affected by this last consideration, for when we went to Hove she was a wealthy woman: in the previous year, and two months before his death, she had been reconciled with her father, who, twenty years before, had disinherited her when she left his comfortable home to go on the stage.

At the time of which I write she was still comparatively young – about forty-two – with small hands, slender ankles

and a long narrow head set aristocratically on a straight neck. Her eyes were large, and nearly black.

It always puzzled me why Father chose her and, having chosen, why she accepted him – they were so different. He was nearly twenty years older and had lived most of his life with two maiden sisters. When they met he was making a survey of metal deposits in a piece of out-of-the-way country near Hull. He must have pitied the tired young actress who, late one Sunday night, was admitted to his boarding-house by a reluctant landlady because the hotels were full – or he may have been fascinated by her contrast with his sisters. On her side, his calmness and silences must have appealed to her.

Within a year of their marriage I was born, and two years later Tim arrived. Two years afterwards Father's work took him abroad – to the Gold Coast – but Mother would not go with him: this was the first big difficulty in their marriage, I have been told. Father, reserved and silent, left with few words and was away for four years.

Until my grandfather died Mother managed to live within the income Father provided, but the day she came into her own money her extravagance burst out like a flood. She took the house at Hove, engaged five servants and a nurse for us and entertained recklessly. Although motoring was then a luxury, she bought a large car.

There was something terribly pathetic about Mother: she became the victim of those members of once noble families who fetch up at south coast watering-places, and who play their part for anyone willing to pay. Many were the evenings during that spring when Tim and I, lying in bed in our room

at the top of the house, were wakened by the throb of motor-cars and the high laughter of some of Mother's departing friends. Among the voices we could hear hers – quick and over-eager – asking them to come again. As the cars turned beneath the trees their lamps flashed across the moulded ceiling, and after they had gone and Mother had come into the house, the night would grow suddenly quiet, except for a late bus hurrying back to its depot along the empty front.

Because the beach was stony and unfit for children (a cause of annoyance to Father when he returned home that summer) we used to play in the gardens opposite. Tim amused himself with a big red ball, while Nurse sat with a novel. I can never think about this time in my life without a sinking of the heart. The quiet, sunny garden symbolises a great emptiness. Every now and again I used to look up at the long, elegant windows of the house which, although beautiful, could give me nothing that really mattered. Mother scarcely ever joined us. Sometimes she came in for a few minutes when she returned home for lunch, but she was seldom alone.

It was that summer, during the first week in July, that Mr Patton first came to the house. He was inclined to be corpulent, and gentle – a bachelor. He had travelled all over Europe making a collection of miniatures which, I believe, is now famous. There was a kindness about him which made him, of all Mother's friends, the one we liked the most. His skin was pink and soft, and he wore light suits always adorned with a dark red buttonhole. Generally he brought us a box of sweets, and sometimes Mother allowed us to have tea with them in the drawing-room upstairs. While Mr Patton told us a

fairy story which continued from one tea-party to the next, Mother, beside the tea-set of apple-green and gold, would listen with her hands behind her head.

In the late summer Father came home. Mr Patton, who had now become almost the only visitor to the house, kept away for some days.

He arrived one wet afternoon just before tea. The wind was fierce that day and the paddle-boat, going down-Channel against the white breakers, let out a taper of black smoke against the grey sea. Nurse took us up to the drawing-room.

He stood with his back to the gilt mirror above the mantel, his hands behind him and his thin head bent over. He was greyer and narrower. He found it difficult to be natural with us and could manage only a swift pat on the tops of our heads. During tea Mother seemed to be nervous: she spoke rapidly and smiled continually. Her hair, generally piled up, had been demurely parted in the middle and drawn back.

Within a few days Mr Patton had resumed his visits. After dinner he would sit with Mother and Father at the open window of the drawing-room. I do not think the men spoke much to each other – they had so little in common. Mother seemed to do all the talking and then, in a deep silence, would turn her head toward the lighted promenade.

Then one evening – I have never managed to forget it – Mother and Mr Patton went out in the warm dusk for a walk. From my bed I heard the front door bang and Mr Patton's low, friendly voice followed by Mother's high laugh. The scent of Mr Patton's cigar reached into the bedroom. I heard them going down the road, the ring of Mother's heels

growing fainter. I lay without moving, looking on to the gently stirring trees outside.

At eleven o'clock Father came to bed. Half an hour later Mother returned. She was alone. After the front door had shut behind her I heard her on the stairs and a moment later she was in our room. For some reason which I have always regretted, I kept my head on my pillow and pretended to be asleep.

She came over to us. Tim stirred and she stopped dead. But as we remained quiet, she gently drew up the painted nursery chair between the beds and sat for a long while staring at us.

Next morning she took us on the promenade. She held our hands and asked us a lot of questions. She spoke rapidly, and laughed at anything we meant to be funny. At lunch she was silent. Father, wearing a high collar and a grey cravat, took no notice of us. Afterwards we went upstairs to rest.

We did not see Mr Patton after that. In fact, he never again came to the house. Four days later Father went for a long walk on the Downs and since it was a wild day with rain in the air Nurse took us for a brisk walk down to Portslade. It was too windy to play with the ball and we were soon covered in seaspray. When we returned home for lunch Mother was not there.

After tea Father came in. He came straight to the nursery and asked us if we knew where she was. His voice was high and seemed to falter. My heart dropped at the sight of his worn, thin face and anxious eyes. But he said nothing until the following morning, when he called us into the drawing-room,

after breakfast. There he told us, as we stood on either side of Nurse, that Mother had left us. I can still see his thin neck and bent shoulders in the mirror behind. She had left what money remained to Tim and me but, standing in the now hollow room, I was aware only of bewilderment and betrayal.

* * *

After Father had divorced her he did not go away again. He grew even more silent and remote, and left the management of our affairs to his sister, Frances, who came to live with us. We saw Mother only once more. On our way home from school about a year later, she came out of one of the shelters on the promenade and approached us hesitantly. She was thinner, and her eyes seemed brighter. For a moment I could do nothing but, as the tears came into her eyes, I dropped my satchel and flung my arms round her, while Tim stamped his boots on the pavement, making little shrieks of joy.

She turned us round and walked some of the way back, gripping our hands fiercely and asking us questions, one after the other. She was very excited and her voice kept rising.

But when we reached the entrance to the terrace she stopped.

'I can't come any further.'

She sounded frightened.

'But you're coming home?' I said. I can never describe the desolation which came over me then.

'I have made you late for lunch,' faltered Mother, panic in her eyes. 'Whatever will they say!'

Tim now clung to her arm.

'You're not going away again?'

This was too much for her. She burst out crying and pushed us away from her. Hardly knowing what she did she came back and kissed us both frantically, unable to look at us, and then turned away with a sob which came from low down in her throat. As she half ran down the road, leaving us staring after her, she did not look back.

The house, austere and lovely in the pale sunshine, was all that now remained. But I remember that, as we entered, the shadows in the hall seemed to have deepened – the staircase led to an empty drawing-room. Thereafter I dared not look too long at the big windows, closed because of the approach of winter, nor at the gilt mirror which reflected only my peaky face and the empty wall beyond.

In due course Mr Patton married Mother and they went to live in Switzerland. Four years later she died suddenly, at Montreux. It was a great shock, for she was still comparatively young. Father, as he grew older, finally lost all contact with us. When I was sixteen he had a stroke and died. Aunt Frances gave up the house and we went to live with Father's other sister in the country.

And now this war has changed everything again. Tim is married, but has been sent to Egypt, and I am nursing in a big hospital in London. During the great blitzes I worked day and night and, finally, was sent away for a rest. I went to Brighton.

While there I walked down the promenade to Hove. The sight of the buildings, like palaces in the yellow light, brought

back to me the old agony of Mother's going. And then, turning by the spring trees, into the terrace, I pulled up short: in that even row of beautiful houses there was a rent like a drawn tooth.

One evening in the winter of 1940 – quite early, about six – a bomb fell there, and all that is left of the house where we lived is a heap of rubble in which you can distinguish nothing except a little piece of the wrought-iron banister which used to be on either side of the curved staircase.

NO CHANGE

Elisabeth was the neater of the two. She was taller and had a sedate air which Millicent lacked. They both looked lovely, but had been lovelier; they were known in the town as 'the Misses Blake', never 'the Miss Blakes'.

Elisabeth undertook the shopping, Millicent the housekeeping. They kept a maid of forty-three, named Edith, who was devoted to them. The three women lived in a large, late-Victorian house on the outskirts of the town and, what with the business of running jumble sales, organising working parties for the women and lending a hand at the fêtes and bazaars which came their way, they were nearly always occupied. Sometimes they went to point-to-points in the country districts, although it was not their habit to hunt. On these occasions they wore tweeds and went in a navy blue two-seater driven by Millicent, who was more car-minded than Elisabeth.

There was a brother who had gone to India, in jute, while still a boy. His departure had made an old man of their father and when, quite soon after, he died, the sisters felt, but would never admit, that Ralph had been selfish to go off and leave them like that.

Besides, it would have been nice to have a man about the house.

When the baker called, Edith occasionally allowed herself to discuss the Misses Blake with an outsider. Why had neither married? They were well off, lovely to look at, and still reasonably young. She was both puzzled and irritated.

'Waste of two good lives,' she sometimes said.

When, one day, a letter with an Indian postmark arrived at the house, she was deeply curious. Ralph had ceased writing long ago, so completely had he made his life out there. She propped the letter on Miss Elisabeth's breakfast tray and went upstairs. All correspondence addressed to them both she took to Elisabeth; Millicent was scatter-brained when letters had to be answered.

Elisabeth, who had been reading Scott already for an hour, took the letter and read it carefully while Edith took longer than usual at the curtains. She then got out of bed, put on her pink dressing-gown, and went into the next room where Millicent lay asleep.

'A letter from Ralph,' Edith heard. 'A friend of his – Arthur Somerton – has left Bombay by now and is coming to visit us.'

'How pleasant,' murmured Millicent, dreamily. 'What are you going to do about it?'

'We shall ask him to dinner, naturally.'

When he came, he hung his black overcoat and white scarf in the cloakroom and washed his hands carefully at the basin. They were long and bloodless, tanned and a little shrivelled

10

on the backs. As Millicent took his hand she felt the hard, cold skin against her own. Ralph had said something about archaeology. Digging up old pots all his life, she thought.

Elisabeth sat at the head of the table; Millicent and their visitor on either side. Arthur Somerton could not remember when he had last met anyone so composed and gentle as Elisabeth. It was a long time since he had been in England, he told himself, taking up his fish knife and fork. Too long. If he didn't look out he'd get out of touch altogether.

It was then that Millicent offered him the cruet and he noticed how fresh and friendly she looked, her eyes alight and inquiring, her hair a little untidy but thick and lively. A calm, intense pleasure spread over him to be sitting there with these two women in their quiet Victorian house, with the silver shining on the mahogany sideboard behind. It was worth coming so far out of his way to do this. And Ralph had said: 'You'd better look them up if you go to the Midlands. I can't guarantee you'll like them. I've not seen them for years but I expect the place is the same as when I was there. They wouldn't change much.'

I can't guarantee you'll like them!

And they were two of the loveliest people he had ever met!

His shining, covert glance was not lost to either of them. As Millicent cracked a walnut she knew he watched her closely, his eyes taking in every movement, from her little frown as the nut refused to splinter, to her firm, ringless hands. In the drawing-room he helped Elisabeth reach for a book on the Indus. His bones cracked a little and they all laughed good-naturedly. He watched Elisabeth through his cigar smoke (they

had no cigarettes) and noticed how carefully she returned her coffee cup to its saucer.

How like Ralph never to have thought of them and then suddenly to have sent them this man; it was like sending a case of tea or a set of ebony elephants, almost without thinking. Such a nice person; so un-Ralphlike, so cultured.

Until nearly midnight he kept them interested with descriptions of his life in the East. He presented to them a picture of a scorched, crowded country, holding none of the calmer pleasures he so much preferred and which, he said, it was possible to find in England and even, though in a lesser way, in the Midlands.

'I hope the next trip will be my last before I finally decide to settle in England,' he said, thoughtfully, flicking his cigar ash into the fire. 'And I think,' he added luxuriously, 'I deserve it.'

Millicent regarded him keenly.

His face was thin, almost cadaverous. Would he find it so easy to start life all over again?

He did not leave until after midnight and kept them long in the hall with one tale of India after another. Finally, he shook them both warmly by the hand.

'I shall come again,' he said, and added, 'that is – if I may?' He waited eagerly, his head thrust forward, for their response.

'We shall be very pleased if you do,' said Elisabeth.

The two women returned to the drawing-room and stood by the dying fire. Elisabeth made a pretence of warming her hands.

As his car passed the window on its way into the road the sisters looked at each other interrogatively. Without speaking they understood each other perfectly.

'He likes us both – you realise?' Millicent said at last.

Elisabeth smiled.

'Either of us would do.'

After some moments' silence, Millicent asked:

'Well, and what are we going to do?'

'Yes. What are we going to do?'

Millicent looked over her shoulder into the dim shadows of the room. The pictures shone faintly; the photograph of their father on the top of the piano watched them.

'I don't think I shall do anything.'

'Nor I.'

The fire grew dimmer, greyer.

'How like Ralph,' said Elisabeth.

MISS CARMICHAEL'S BED

As she snuffed out the candle and drew the fresh sheets up to her chin the tang of the sea was in the room; against the ceiling flickered the reflection of the moonlit water under the window. From her pillow she could see the mainland: the harbour wall lit by the row of lights under the hotel, and two figures standing motionless at the head of the causeway.

Unable to sleep, she lay thinking of the journey which had culminated in her arrival at this house to take up the duties of housekeeper. She remembered Paddington at nine in the morning, thronged with schoolchildren returning after the summer holidays, and the packed railway carriage as far as Swindon. After that she had travelled in comfort. Each time the train stopped the air seemed to have grown heavier and the vegetation stronger; a *burr* appeared in the voices of the porters as they called out the names of the stations.

At 4.20 she changed lines. As the tiny engine puffed towards the sea a pink sky appeared behind groves of ilex trees. She drew Miss Carmichael's letter from her handbag and read it again. Careful instructions for the journey were written in purplish-black ink of the kind which faded; she pictured a woman of about sixty-five, gaunt and tall, wearing probably a boned lace collar and a cameo brooch, but beyond that she

could not go. The train halted at a small station in a deep valley and she looked out. As Miss Carmichael had written, Willis was there with his taxi to meet her. He came forward briskly, a youngish, clean-shaven man in a light trench-coat.

It was in coloured twilight that she first saw the island, like a bulging map below them. It was deep violet, and the stones and seaweed on the causeway were viridian and pink. Mary Hackett was not given to wonderment but the sight took her breath away.

She touched Willis on the shoulder with her umbrella. 'How beautiful,' she said.

'Everyone likes this bit,' he called back.

They drew up at the hotel. A waiter opened the door of the car.

'How's the tide, Bert?' Willis inquired.

'Give it twenty minutes,' the man answered.

She went into the lounge and ordered tea. From the window she could see the thinly scattered, whitewashed houses on the island and one or two boats at their moorings in the harbour like black shells on the almost white water; to the right lay the dark hills of the mainland. As she sipped her tea a few lights appeared on the island opposite.

Willis came for her. She paid her bill and followed him. A porter from the hotel had her luggage on a handcart and was trundling it down the beach. They set off across the causeway, with the quiet sea on either side.

The sparse lights ahead and the stillness of the evening made her shudder a little, but the presence of Willis, who had lit a cigarette, was reassuring.

'You see that light farthest on the point,' he said, 'That's Miss Carmichael's.'

She could make out the dark shape of the house on a little hill. They were soon to meet, she and Hannah Carmichael. They would hit it off or they would not, she told herself.

As if he knew her thoughts he said, 'I hope you'll get on well with Miss Carmichael, miss. Nobody knows much about her, although she's been here for nearly thirty years.'

'Does she live alone?' Mary asked.

'A coastguard's wife "does" for her, but she never has visitors from one year's end to another.'

'How old is she?'

'In the sixties.'

When the little procession reached the other side she felt as if the island closed round her and prevented her retreat. She was unused to such feelings and, breathing deeply, she took off her silk scarf. The air was oppressive and scented heavily with the sea.

Miss Carmichael's house was square with tall windows and a slate roof which already shone with the rising moon. Like most houses along that coast it had been built in 1860 or thereabouts. A small oil-lamp in the hall sent a beam through the coloured fan-light above the door. Below the stone wall in front lay the sea; dark rocks like seals appeared and receded in the scarcely perceptible swell of the water.

'I hope you'll be all right, miss,' said Willis in a fatherly tone as he helped the porter unload her luggage in the porch. As they went off their footsteps rang against the side of the house.

She knocked.

The door was answered by a stoutish woman in her thirties. 'Are you Miss Hackett?' she asked. 'Come in. Miss Carmichael is expecting you.'

She led her into a front room, lit dimly by an oil-lamp.

'I'll tell her you're here,' she said, and withdrew.

Mary Hackett looked about her. A set of six Victorian chairs faced each other across a broad dining-table. Two blurred photographs of a middle-aged lady and gentleman hung above the fireplace which had been filled by a pale fern in a copper pot. She went to the uncurtained window and putting her hand to the pane looked on to the sea.

At that moment someone entered the room.

She turned quickly. Miss Carmichael was holding the back of a chair with long bony hands. In the poor light Mary observed a narrow, unsmiling and unusually pale face in a frame of thick dark hair (which turned out later to be a wig), black, sharp eyes, and winged nostrils. Her people must have been well-to-do tradespeople in Wales for when she spoke her voice was touched by a Welsh accent.

'Good evening, Miss Hackett.'

Mary went forward with her hand out. Miss Carmichael took it without altering her expression.

'I am glad you have come. But before going further we must understand one another.' She drew out two chairs from the table. 'Sit down, please.'

Mary did so, slowly.

'Mrs Trefoyle is preparing you a meal, but before you go to it there are one or two things I want you to know. You may not wish to stay here when you have heard them.'

Her voice was sombre and her face looked as if she never smiled.

'I have lived alone in this house for twenty-eight years. Apart from Mrs Trefoyle, who comes in every day to clean up and do the cooking, no one comes near me. I do not care for other people and wish only to be left alone. In fact, I am what my dear father called a misanthropist.' Her eyes went to the darkened window. 'My only friends are the gulls which come here to be fed.'

Mary watched the other's thin face and dark, fierce eyes. All connection with the long train journey had gone; she had been absorbed into the stone house and the ill-lit room, closed round by the sea.

'It is not from choice that I want to engage you as my housekeeper,' the other went on. 'Rather, it is the last thing I would wish. But it has been God's will to afflict my health,' she studied her hands finger by finger, 'my health is not good. Mrs Trefoyle has told me that unless somebody lives here with me she will go. It is the fear of having to engage someone from the island (all of whom I know and detest) which has driven me to it. I received many letters in answer to my advertisement, but yours was the most satisfactory: you sounded sensible and practical. I am glad to see that you are in your late thirties and appear to be experienced – not given to stupidity or excessive imagination. If you wish to stay here under these conditions you can do so, but you must please yourself. Perhaps you will be good enough to decide.'

She stopped abruptly and stared almost without breathing at her hands.

Mary considered her. The suddenness of the request unnerved her a little. She looked at her handbag and then at her feet. A long sighing wave washed the rocks: the tide had turned.

She had come so far – why not stay? She had trained as a nurse and could deal with sick people. She had no other job to go to and needed a change; the sea air would do her good. From somewhere in the house a cheerful clock beat the time flatly.

She looked up. 'Thank you. I should like to stay.'

Miss Carmichael made no sign: it seemed the same to her whether Mary stayed or went. She rose.

'Very well. Let me add that I do not wish this conversation to be referred to again. You will have very little to do: you will attend me only when I am ill. We shall take as little notice of each other as possible, and will eat separately.'

She went to the door.

'Mrs Trefoyle will show you to your room. Good night.'

She crossed the little hall into another sitting-room and closed the door after her.

Mrs Trefoyle had prepared a cold meal in the kitchen. 'I'm glad you've come here, Miss Hackett,' she said, pouring out very strong tea. 'The mistress is difficult at times. I've stood it for some years but now it's beginning to tell on my nerves.' She looked up. 'Did she tell you what her illness was?'

Mary was munching a radish. She shook her head.

'She's an epileptic,' said Mrs Trefoyle, watching her closely.

What was there in that? Mary asked herself. To look after an epileptic patient was not more exacting than a rheumatic

one. She drank her tea gratefully, tired now after the long journey.

At nine o'clock Mrs Trefoyle went home. On her way to bed Mary tapped at the door of Miss Carmichael's sitting-room, but received no answer: she had already gone upstairs. When she got to her own room she found that Mrs Trefoyle had lighted the candle and a hot-water bottle was in the bed. Through the window came the fresh salt air.

2

Mrs Trefoyle called her at seven.

As she passed Miss Carmichael's room she noticed, through the half-opened door, a huge double bed. It was the largest box-bed she had ever seen. It was neatly made and covered with a white lace counterpane. A night-dress case, covered with embroidered roses, lay on the high pillow. She would have liked to step into the room and have a quick look round but she was afraid Miss Carmichael was there.

Miss Carmichael, however, was already downstairs.

At half-past nine Mary crossed by ferry to the mainland for the morning's shopping. As she waited for the man to row slowly over to take her back she lifted a handful of sand and let it trickle through her fingers. Small white clouds were clustering on the horizon and a gust of wind made trellis patterns on the sea. It was very nice here. She felt sure she would like her new job despite the strangeness of her employer.

3

It was not until Mary had been there a week that Miss Carmichael was taken ill. She was having tea in the kitchen with Mrs Trefoyle when the handbell rang in the sitting-room.

'You'd better go quickly, miss. It sounds as if she's bad.'

Mary found Miss Carmichael in the armchair and the handbell on its side on the floor. She helped her gently to the ground and afterwards they put her to bed. As Mary drew back the counterpane the lower part of the bed came to view.

'This is a huge bed,' she murmured.

Mrs Trefoyle nodded. 'She had it made for her many years ago. She'll never allow me to so much as touch it. I'm not allowed to do out the room either.'

Mary went to the window. The stones of the causeway were ochre in the sunlight.

'I wonder what she keeps in it?' she thought.

4

After she had been there two months Miss Carmichael invited her into her sitting-room, and soon it became her habit to go there in the evenings. Although scarcely a word passed between the two women, it was pleasant to knit and read by the leaping fire while the storms of winter shook the little house. But not once did Miss Carmichael divulge anything further about herself. There were times when her fixed, brooding eyes considered Mary in silence, as if she had something she was

about to say, but Mary made no effort to lead her on, and perhaps that was why Miss Carmichael invited her company.

5

When the spring came the only difference in the lives of the three women was that Mrs Trefoyle was pregnant and could no longer lift heavy weights.

One afternoon Miss Carmichael gave a sign of her growing trust in Mary by sending her upstairs for her spectacles which had been left on the dressing-table.

As Mary was about to leave the room she noticed that the edge of the counterpane was caught up between the lid and the bottom of the bed. She tugged it sharply but it would not come away. Turning her back to the door and half-burying her head in the feather mattress she caught hold of the two leather handles on the lid. She was just about to lift it a little when a fierce voice spoke behind her:

'How dare you touch that bed!'

Miss Carmichael was in the doorway, her face thinner and paler than ever, her eyes piercingly black.

Mary straightened up.

'I am extremely sorry, Miss Carmichael. I set the counterpane to rights.'

'Kindly leave this room.'

'As you wish,' Mary answered. When she reached the kitchen she was trembling violently.

That evening she was not invited to the sitting-room and it was a long while before she went there again.

6

After that it became Miss Carmichael's habit to stay in her bedroom, with the door locked, for long stretches at a time. Once when Mary was feeding the gulls she looked back at the house and saw Miss Carmichael's eyes, like circles of ebony in her white face, watching her from the shadowy room behind.

Although Mary thought often of the bed, its secret did not trouble her. On the occasions when Miss Carmichael had a fit and they put her to bed they disturbed nothing in the room. Mrs Trefoyle was inclined to view it all in a superstitious light.

'She's queerer than she was,' she said often. 'I hope the baby won't be affected by it all.'

But the child was born apparently none the worse. During Mrs Trefoyle's convalescence Mary was busy with the house.

Miss Carmichael's attacks had grown more frequent and she was obliged to manage her single-handed, often sitting with her for a long while afterwards, watching her with care.

7

When autumn came Mary began to feel the strain, but it was not until Willis drew her attention to it by a quizzical 'You're not looking well, miss – if you don't mind me saying,' that she felt quite done up.

A few days later she asked Miss Carmichael if she could take a holiday.

She received the request in silence but that evening as Mary was filling the bottles she joined her in the kitchen.

'If you must go away for a time, you must,' her voice was stony. 'It will be awkward. In fact, we – I – will miss you very much, Miss Hackett.'

She turned and left the room abruptly. Mary watched her retreating back, her gently sloping shoulders and her thin elbows pressed against her sides.

Before it was light next morning Mary heard Miss Carmichael moving about in her room. When she went downstairs she found her in the narrow hall taking an umbrella out of the rack; she was wearing a plain black dress Mary had not seen before.

'I am going to Plymouth for the day,' she said. 'I expect to return by the three-thirty train.'

Mary was startled. She had not known Miss Carmichael leave the island.

'May I go with you?'

'No, thank you,' the other replied, putting on her green mackintosh.

Mary went to the front door and looked out. The tide was fairly full and the light was breaking a faint canary yellow, windswept and stormy.

'I don't think I should go if I were you,' she said anxiously.

Miss Carmichael made no reply. She carefully buttoned up her mackintosh.

'Let me go with you,' Mary asked again, but without being answered.

When Miss Carmichael opened the front door the wind

made the pictures swing on the walls. She paused and for a moment looked at the dark green waves which rose and fell in front of her, and then without another word, she went down the steep path to the landing stage.

Fifteen minutes later Mary could see from her bedroom window the ferryman rowing his boat gingerly against the breakers, Miss Carmichael, stiff and thin in her green mackintosh, sitting bolt upright in the stern.

By lunchtime a gale was blowing. She and Mrs Trefoyle ate their meal in silence and afterwards Mrs Trefoyle went home.

At about three o'clock Mary went to the window. The tide was almost out, and fan-shaped waves, backed by the wind, were spreading over the causeway. It was impossible to get to the island at present. 'She may have to stay the night at the hotel,' she thought.

She pictured her in one of the bedrooms on the other side of the water, but the idea was preposterous. Miss Carmichael could never be in any bed but her own.

Her bed! It was with a violent shock that she remembered the mystery of the brown box upstairs.

Now that the house was empty what would prevent her from discovering its secret once and for all? Guiltily she went into the kitchen to make sure that Mrs Trefoyle had gone home and therefore would not hear her if she went upstairs, but the sight of the crockery neatly laid for tea and the honest tick of the alarm clock checked her, and she returned to the sitting-room. She took up the *Argus* and tried to read, but now her attention could not be regulated: her mind returned

continually to the thought of the bed in Miss Carmichael's room.

At half-past four she was uneasy. Supposing something had happened to Miss Carmichael while she was in Plymouth? Instead of making tea she went to the front door. The wind nearly blew her over as she struggled to the stone wall and peered into the needle points of spray which were torn from the breast of the sea; fierce, shallow waves swirled and groaned among the rocks. The tide was turning.

On the mainland the hotel stood the buffeting of the wind. A light glimmered in the lounge. Perhaps at this moment Miss Carmichael was sitting there, resigned to the idea of staying there the night. The sky was a muddy yellow. She would not come now.

There would be no one in Miss Carmichael's bed tonight.

Again the pang of curiosity and fear! She shivered, crossed her arms and fled indoors. She leaned for a moment against the wall in the narrow, dark hall, her heart leaping, her skin cold.

Where would be the harm of looking into the box beneath Miss Carmichael's bed?

The empty hall and the stairs seemed to encourage and beckon her. She might as well get it over and done with.

She climbed the stairs, one hand on the rail, the other over her heart. She had formed no theory of what the bed contained – if it contained anything. Her longing to know was unreasonable and guilty.

She opened the door of the room and went in. The fading, stormy light fell on the bed so that the embroidered roses on

the night-dress case seemed almost to be real. She had but to lift the lid and all would be known.

She reached down swiftly and turned back the counter-pane; the great brown box-bed was exposed to view. Briskly she took hold of the handles and was just about to heave up the lid when the window behind her rattled so much with the wind that it was as if someone had thrown a bundle of wet seaweed against it.

With a beating heart she went to the window and looked out. Broken clouds drifted inland; every now and then the sea broke smoothly over the black and glistening causeway.

In the failing light she made out a little knot of people standing on the far beach. Just then a figure broke away and came running down to the causeway. She rubbed the glass and peered out: what was it going to do? To her dismay she recognised the tall frame, the mackintosh and the umbrella. Miss Carmichael! Two people detached themselves from the group and came after her, but she only ran the faster. Miss Carmichael was endeavouring to cross the causeway by foot in a violent storm! Mary's hands went to her throat. 'Stop her, somebody,' she called thinly, from behind the window.

Someone made as though to catch her by the arm but stopped still as a wave ran up the beach. She started off along the causeway with the waters swirling around her ankles. For a moment it looked as if she had lost her balance on the slip-pery stones and would be drawn into the sea, but she struggled on. By now she was running, her umbrella in the air.

'Go back. For heaven's sake, *go back*,' Mary hissed, rubbing on the window with frantic fingers.

Above Miss Carmichael's head she saw a great roller driving down the narrow strip between the island and the mainland. It drove faster as it came. Mary screamed as she watched what the running woman had not seen.

'For God's sake, look out!' she yelled.

In the next second the roller plunged across the causeway, breaking into thousands of circular, tearing eddies, and continued on its wild way into the sea beyond.

When the causeway cleared it was black and empty. Mary stared at the dark water – for a moment an arm was seen, stuck out at an impossible angle, but afterwards she could not be sure whether she had seen or only fancied it.

8

Willis and three fishermen from lower down the coast brought her body in next morning. There was seaweed in her hair. They laid her on the big bed and she was there for three days until they buried her. Although Mary went in and out of the room she never once thought of the mystery of the bed.

At the inquest no one wondered how she came to be in Miss Carmichael's room and so had witnessed the tragedy. She, too, had almost forgotten.

At the funeral in the island chapel there were three other mourners: a nephew and his wife from Swansea, and a short, stocky lawyer in striped trousers from Plymouth. After the ceremony Mary made tea and later the lawyer read out the will.

The nephew came in for the house, some Consols, an interest in an unproductive Welsh mine and the balance on deposit. He was also to have the furniture. But there was a codicil.

The lawyer took off his glasses and rubbed his eyes. 'Miss Carmichael came to me the day of her – of the disaster, to make this amendment' – the nephew and his wife exchanged glances – 'It concerns you, Miss Hackett.' He gave her his full gaze. 'She has bequeathed the "big bed and all therein contained to Mary Hackett, Spinster, at present residing with me as my housekeeper." She was particularly anxious that this should be done there and then.'

The nephew's wife smiled graciously. 'How nice for you,' she said relieved.

The bed! It was as though Miss Carmichael had known of her guilty action in going to the room.

They all beamed at her. The nephew said:

'It's worth quite a bit, that bed. I expect the hotel would buy it from you.'

'I wonder what's inside it,' the wife said, dubiously.

'Let's go up and find out,' he said eagerly.

Mary did not stir.

'I think – I think I would prefer to wait,' she said, quietly.

The nephew was a little abashed. 'Just as you please.'

She felt the least she could do now to lay that thin ghost was to learn the secret alone.

9

The lawyer departed early, for the gale still blew (though not so furiously). After a thorough examination of the house and furniture the nephew and his wife left for the mainland where they were staying the night.

Mary watched them go off in the gathering dark. As soon as the small light of the ferry-boat reached mid-channel she lit a candle and went to Miss Carmichael's room.

Now that the body had gone she was aware of the silence and emptiness of the room – this sanctuary of Miss Carmichael. She crossed to the bed: the embroidered night-dress case was askew on the pillow.

With her heart pounding she bent down and turned aside the counterpane. The leather handles came to view. She grasped them and pulled.

The lid was so heavy that she wondered how Miss Carmichael had managed it alone. Without looking inside she levered her back beneath it and groped with her hand for something to prop it up with. She found a piece of wood in one corner and made it secure. Very carefully she balanced the candle on the edge.

Tremblingly she peered in. A white dust-sheet covered it from end to end. All over the surface was broken by lumps and points: little hills and valleys made by what it concealed. She raised one end and drew it back with bated breath, until the whole dark cavern of the bed box was disclosed.

Carefully she raised the candle above her head and peered closely at the disordered array of objects which lay within; a

jumble of oddments so varied that many she had never seen before were mixed with others so commonplace that each must have contained a network of everyday memories, and all lying as if they had been thrown in from a distance. There were broken bits of jewellery, pinchbeck lockets stained with plaited hair; coins from Victoria's jubilee, gold sovereigns tumbled here and there; a penny whistle, even a sardine-tin opener; a girl's silk dress rolled into a ball; stamped china from Welsh watering-places; a feather from a hat, a set of false teeth, a rabbit's foot, a fan, a tortoiseshell comb, some pebbles, an oyster shell; in one corner lay a linnet's nest.

Mary knelt down before the objects. The happy light of the candle leaped over these relics of a woman's life, dancing carelessly over the symbols of the loneliness of Miss Carmichael's soul.

The candle burnt down and Mary Hackett continued to kneel, staring into the black shadows of the box under the bed. Every now and then she let out a little sob.

THE LAND GIRL

I have Jersey cream for breakfast here on the farm. It is thick enough to spread on my porridge. Unfortunately, there is not enough sugar to go with it because of the rationing, which is rather a curse. What I'd like would be oceans of brown sugar crystals of the kind we used to have at my guardian's. As it is, I have to take it surreptitiously when Mrs Farrant goes to the kitchen for the kettle. She's very severe and down on land girls altogether. She's also against me because I'm a 'lady', or I am when compared with her. She's a hard-bitten, crusty, thin woman and I don't think she and her husband get on particularly well together. She never calls him by his name or anything else, and refers to him as 'Mr Farrant'.

They don't half work the land girls. You are expected to do a man's work right enough. Not that I mind: it's fun being out in the open all day, even if it is blasted cold. Today we fallowed a field the size of the hall at college and it took five hours. About mid-afternoon Mr Farrant came over and gave me a cigarette. I'm not allowed to smoke at the farmhouse because of Mrs F, so I have one now and again in the fields. It's decent of him to understand. I should say he's a man of about fifty-six, tall, very thin and his face is lined with tiny red veins.

He has whitish hair and blue, amused eyes. I wish he wouldn't wear leather gaiters: they make his legs look far too thin.

'We'll make you into a farmer yet, Miss Una,' he said.

I laughed at the idea. If there weren't a war on I'd never be doing landwork. I don't believe I've got the patience. Farming is a dull game: you have to wait so long for things to grow. I like action. It was that which got me expelled from school – I used to sneak into the town to buy sweets after 'lights-out'. I've also got strong feelings, with decided likes and dislikes. Which reminds me, I don't think I'm going to like Mrs F at all.

There's a thick frost today. Miller, the cowman, says it went down to 27 degrees last night. I was late for breakfast because it was so hard getting out of bed. Mr Farrant was on the farm and Mrs F was busy in the scullery. It was quite nice to eat alone. I didn't have to be endlessly on my best behaviour. Believe me I was in a rage when I discovered that Mrs F had left only a teaspoonful of sugar in the bowl for both tea and porridge. Mean old pig! I thought. I'll pay you out. Before I went on the farm I upset my tea over the tablecloth.

Miller was detailed for two hours to teach me how to manage the tractor. When the weather breaks we'll be busy. Miller is a bad teacher, or I'm a dud. I expect I shall understand it in time.

Mr Farrant gave me my lesson this morning. He explains things very well. He took the whole carburettor to pieces and showed me how it worked.

The weather is still mid-winter. Today I felt very bored, going up and down among the cabbages. If the war goes on much longer I shall be sick of this game. Nobody of my own age to talk to, only the farmhands and their wives, and I bet they laugh and imitate me behind my back. To tell the truth I don't feel I'm all that popular, and this makes me seem affected. Am beginning to wonder why I ever came here at all.

This morning Mr Farrant took me in his gig to market. The town looked like a Christmas card by Raphael Tuck: people were climbing the hill bent double for fear of falling on the ice, and one or two women wore red woollen caps with lipstick to match.

I enjoy going around with Mr Farrant. He's a nice old boy and treats me well. He was shy at first about taking me into the Drovers because he said I was a lady. It was very hot and farmerish in there. I must say I enjoyed drinking a glass of good old brown ale with the locals. These togs, breeches and coat etc, are very comfortable. Thank goodness I don't bulge out in the wrong places.

When we got home Mrs F didn't seem particularly pleased to see us. She spilled my tea pouring it out, so I refused to thank her for it. When she went to lock up the fowls I am afraid I pulled a face at Mr Farrant, but he didn't seem to mind.

There has been another fall of snow. My room is in the attic and after Mr Farrant called me to get up I lay quite a while looking at it reflected on the ceiling.

Practically all day I was clambering about with Miller searching for a pair of ewes which have lambed too early. After we'd found them Mrs Miller made tea for us at their cottage. It was the queerest place inside. The 'parlour' was fixed from top to bottom with pictures of the seaside, and china 'gifts', mostly from Brighton. She was very pleasant and had only two teeth in the top front. I wonder what happened to the others. Miller is a robust, earnest sort of fellow, and good-looking, if you like the earthy type.

Mrs Farrant made a scene today. I have come to loathe her. When I came in I shook off all the snow I could in the scullery before going into the sitting-room. Mr Farrant was doing accounts. I could see she was in a vile temper: her hair was screwed into a tighter knot than ever.

I sat in an armchair and took up the *Daily Mail*.

Presently she looked across.

'Why didn't you take off your boots?' she said.

Before answering I laid the paper down very deliberately, and looked her over.

'Because I've been out all day on the farm and I'm dog-tired. I shook the snow off as I came in.'

'The snow's all over the carpet, and you'll take off those boots,' she said.

She came and stood over me so menacingly that my gore rose.

'My good woman,' I said. 'I haven't taken up farming to be ordered about by you.'

'This is my house and I'll be obeyed in it.'

'No one could mistake that,' I replied curtly, and I admit I looked meaningly at Mr Farrant.

'You'll kindly leave this room,' Mrs F said. She's certainly got a shrill voice.

'I'm going to, thanks,' I said, and I took the *Daily Mail* with me. As I climbed to my room I brushed off as much snow as I could on the stairs.

When I went down for supper I found Mrs F had gone to bed. Mr Farrant was quiet all through the meal. I am afraid he was upset about it all.

Mrs F is scarcely civil when I address her now. She has also taken to giving me small helpings at meals. When I object she refers to the strict rationing. I don't believe it; we live on a farm where there's plenty of food, and I tell her so.

This morning she had taken away the cream and left no milk for the porridge. She was making her bed upstairs.

I must say I wouldn't like to have a wife like Mrs F.

Last night I went to a Temperance Dance with the Millers. Mrs Miller doesn't dance, so I waggled a toe with him. It was a tiring affair. It's hard to get drunk on lemonade. When we got back to the farm after a three-mile walk through the snow, I found that damned woman had locked me out. All the doors were bolted and the place in darkness. I threw snowballs at Mr Farrant's window – they have separate rooms – and presently he came down, looking very sleepy, poor man, and let me in.

As I passed her door her room was suspiciously quiet. I am

afraid I made no apology for getting him out of bed. He ought never to have married a woman like Flo Farrant.

This morning when I accused her of locking up the house she had the rotten taste to reply, 'Oh, I thought you'd be out all night.'

'What the hell do you mean by that?' I asked.

I think she was frightened because she did not answer.

'Come on,' I said, 'Explain yourself.'

But she wouldn't.

I'm going to get even with her for this.

I spent the whole of today carting hay for the cattle. I can't help thinking of what that bitch said yesterday.

It's open war between Mrs F and me in this house now. I don't know how Mr Farrant can put up with it. I talk only to him. Mrs F and I have put each other into Coventry.

I must think clearly about this evening to know what exactly happened. I admit I did it in an inexplicable, mad moment and I suppose I shall live to regret it, but I do feel Mrs F is entirely to blame for the atmosphere which has grown up between us.

As it was Sunday she caught the early bus into town and went by train to her mother's farm.

She was gone all day.

At lunch-time Mr Farrant and I got on particularly well together. We laughed a good deal at his jokes and he seemed relieved that she was out of the way, and shy that he and I were

alone; which was funny, because around the farm and all the time we are at work he treats me as if I were a sort of refined workman. In the afternoon he dozed, the newspaper over his face and his gaiters off, I was dressed in a frock for a change and feeling no longer a farm labourer.

Over tea we got on still better. I know Mr Farrant likes me quite a lot: I'm sensible and reasonably attractive. I like him in lots of ways. He's friendly and has a sense of humour.

As I poured the tea, sitting in Mrs F's chair, I must admit I was glad she was out of the house for once.

But not a shadow of what happened later entered my head at any time during the afternoon. I wrote some letters to one or two of the people I'd met at the agricultural college and amused Mr Farrant with tales about them. He thought they sounded great jokes.

When supper-time came he insisted that he should prepare it.

'After all, we're both farmers,' he said, 'so why shouldn't I get a meal for a change.'

He opened a tin of tongue and made some sandwiches. The tea was dreadfully strong. Afterwards he smoked some of my cigarettes and told me about his youth. He must have been a lad. Why on earth he had to marry Flo Farrant only the stars can tell.

As she was due on the ten o'clock bus, I decided to go to bed before she arrived. Just before nine-thirty Mr Farrant made the fire up and went into the kitchen to make some tea. While he was gone I put the room to rights, and presently he returned with a thermos and laid it on the table.

It was then that something took possession of me. The sight of the old, chipped thermos on the orange tray and his spent, thin shoulders bent over it, caused my dislike of Mrs Farrant to well up into a sudden storm of hatred. I don't remember ever having experienced such rage and no one can accuse me of being sweet-tempered. I felt choked with hatred. As I watched the nape of his neck I gripped the back of a wooden chair so hard that my hands were bloodless. Yet despite the ferocity of this feeling I don't think it could have lasted a second. I relaxed my grip on the chair and sat down.

He looked up alarmed.

'Are you feeling all right?'

'Yes . . . th-thanks,' I stammered.

'Not ill or anything? You're so white.'

'It must be the heat of the room,' I said and pulled myself together. I got up. 'I'm going to bed.'

'Right you are,' he said. 'I'm turning in, too.'

He went into the kitchen and I heard him stoking the Ideal boiler.

Suddenly my brain began to work at a great speed. Now that I think about it I suppose my subconscious had already worked out a plan. My movements became swift and furtive. I went quickly to the door, looked to right and left in the hall and then, as softly as I could, sped up the stairs. The way I knew what to do next was quite peculiar. I went straight to Mr Farrant's bedroom and switched the light on. His bed was over in the corner. I went straight over and lay on it. I even shook off my shoes as I climbed up – a funny thing to do

when I had only a few moments to spare. I could hear him moving about downstairs and I knew the bus with Mrs Farrant in it would be arriving at any minute. I lay on my back and rolled about from side to side to deepen my impression in the feather mattress. It very soon became disordered. Then I got up, took off a blue Tyrolean brooch I always wear and laid it beside his brushes on the dressing-table. Grabbing my shoes in my hand I made my way onto the landing and up the stairs to the attic.

Once in my own room I stood with my head pressed against the door, listening for the sound of his movements. I heard him lift the lid of the letter-box and let it drop. He paused by the stairs to wind the grandfather clock.

At that moment I heard the bus. It pulled up and then started off noisily. Mrs Farrant was at the gate.

He climbed the stairs softly. I don't think he heard the bus. As he came to the linoleum on the landing his steps grew louder. He crossed to his room and went in.

Hardly breathing I came out of mine and ran stealthily down the stairs. My eyes must have been fixed and frightening. When the front door handle turned I gave a little gasp: nothing must prevent my plan from succeeding. If I were not wrong, Mrs Farrant would say good night to her husband before she drank her tea.

I slipped into his room as quickly and quietly as I could. Once inside I appeared to be in no hurry. He stood in the middle of the room in his shirt sleeves. He appeared not to have noticed the state of the bed, and was staring pensively at his feet. He looked up surprised.

'I'm sorry,' I said, and I can't think what I must have looked like, 'but I've left a brooch on your dressing-table.' I spoke slowly. 'It's a little Austrian brooch my guardian gave me years ago.'

I began to play for time.

'Stupid of me to have left it. There it is – on the little china tray' – I heard footsteps on the stairs – in a slightly higher key I said, 'On the china tray, beside your brushes.'

'Oh,' he said, vaguely, and took it up in his hands. He was stupified and tired. 'I don't quite understand,' he said, and looked down at it in the palm of his hand and then at me. 'How did it get there?'

But I had no need to reply. Mrs Farrant stood in the doorway, her dark clothes part of the shadow in the landing, her face compressed and challenging. She looked at her husband, at the brooch in his hand, at me, and finally, at the disarranged bed.

I don't know what I looked like but I can remember a sensation of rising triumph as I met her eyes. He was too befuddled to know what to say and I made no effort to help him.

I waited an age for her to speak, but she said nothing. Her face became completely expressionless. She looked again at the brooch in Farrant's hand and then turned on her heel. We heard her cross the landing to her own room and close the door sharply behind her.

I must confess I didn't know what to do when he turned and looked at me in a bewildered sort of way. I snatched the brooch from his hand and rushed upstairs to my room.

This morning it is still very cold. As I lay in bed unable to sleep, a good deal of noise was going on in the house below. Eventually I got up and stared out at the outbuildings of this blasted farm. Presently, Miller led the pony out and harnessed him to the gig. Almost at once Mrs Farrant piled it high with some tattered luggage. Without saying anything to Miller she climbed in and jerked the reins. The pony moved forward, through the gate and on to the high road, his breath misty in the frozen morning air. I got cold watching her backview until it was out of sight: the thin body and that frightful bun. That was the last I shall ever see of her, thank God.

After that I dressed and went downstairs.

As I went into the kitchen with a jauntiness I was far from feeling, Mr Farrant was making his own breakfast. He looked up with a numbed expression. I had expected reproaches: it put me off my stroke not to get any.

'She's gone,' he said, wearily, 'Nothing I could say made any difference.'

I said nothing.

Here I am waiting for the bus. It's so cold I have to run up and down beside my suitcases to keep warm. I am in my best clothes, but I do not know where I am going or what I shall do. All I am certain of is: I must get out of that house.

After all, I couldn't stay there alone with Mr Farrant. Even though he's been an awful dear to me he's old enough to be my father. And my life has only just begun.

THE SUMMER HOLIDAY

What insensate heat! Margot dug her elbow into a cool place in the duvet and turned the page of her novel. She had bought it on the day of publication in a bookshop in the rue de Rivoli, eager to possess it, but now she found it almost boring. Presently she laid it face down on the fold of the sheet and turned onto her back. The corners of the room, peacock blue because of the venetian blinds, seemed to her to pulsate with the heat. She shut her eyes and propped her legs on the bedrail. From the café below came the murmur of men's voices. Apparently it mattered little to the black-moustached proprietor of the hotel that the Germans had once more broken loose on France. 'They are so far off. Our army is good,' he had said. He had spent the last three evenings peeling his vine.

It did not seem to matter to Graham either, she reflected, hearing his voice suddenly below. Although to be quite fair to him he had never professed interest in the war. It was run by businessmen and fanatics, he had always said. Hitler – Chamberlain: one a crank, the other a fool! His pointed face peculiarly sallow, Graham would shrug his shoulders – a habit which he had learnt in France and which suited him. She

stretched her arms above her head. What a miracle he had got that job in Paris, and with an American firm. It made them safe. They even had an American passport, because of his mother. It did not matter if the Germans did come.

The voices below grew clearer. She could distinguish Graham's: he was telling a doubtful story slowly. She waited for the climax. In the road a laden cart scrunched by. Soon the sun would slant away from the hotel and her room would freshen. Before dinner she would have a delicious cold sponge-down – and how well they fed you in France! Even after nine months of war. She did not wish ever to return to England. Over here Graham had six weeks' holiday: an English firm would have allowed him no more than three.

She smiled at the thought of how he enjoyed his fishing – bless him! The slow-flowing river, banked by eucalyptus trees was his playground. He looked good in his white linen shorts and navy blue shirt; tanned like a Frenchman – like a native. She was his English wife – fair-skinned, blue-eyed. They were a nice couple, she felt. She dressed well, for they had no children and could therefore afford to. Oh, why on earth had there to be this ridiculous war, she thought savagely, opening wide her eyes.

As she bathed she said to herself: Hitler-Chamberlain. What a couple to get the world so mixed up. Graham was right in his detached, lazy way. Once a Frenchman with very little English, in a railway carriage, had asked him his politics. 'CO, I suppose,' Graham had replied. 'Commanding officer! A militarist?' asked the puzzled Frenchman. 'No, a conchie,' had been Graham's answer, with an amused smile. There was

a good deal of sense in those politics, she chuckled, as she squeezed the sponge out on the nape of her neck. It meant that he and she could holiday in the sun while her sister worried her life out in London, a grass widow with a husband at the front.

She put on her silk dressing-gown and, winding up the venetian blinds, looked out onto the narrow street. The house across the way was now getting the sun, and below, the panama hats of two elderly Frenchmen nodded authoritatively over a bottle of red wine.

'What if the Boches *do* break through?' asked one querulously.

Old and simple, she thought. They'll never get so far.

But over dinner – and the *bifsteak* was particularly good – she asked Graham what would happen if the Germans did come.

He drank his wine slowly.

'They'll never manage it, my sweet,' he smiled, showing his strong teeth. 'Most of what Hitler says is – bunk.'

But that evening a little crowd gathered round the radio and the waiters left their jobs to come and listen against the bar. The announcer read the news with an anxious ring in his voice. Paris was threatened. 'What! Already?' said Graham, 'Pretty quick work.' Thank God for an American passport, thought Margot. Tension rose in the bittersweet-smelling café. 'I think I'll go outside for a few minutes,' said Margot.

She went into the cool street. It was filled with the perfume of flowers opening after the heat of the day. At that moment a car tore by containing two staff officers. It was followed closely

by a motor-cyclist going at full speed. The set expression of their faces sent a chill through her.

What if Paris should fall?

She went back to Graham. He was playing cards with three men.

'You look pale, my sweet,' he said – his accent was faintly American. 'Anything the matter?'

Her heart was heavy and disturbed. 'No – I don't think so.'

They went to bed late. Although it was almost too hot to sleep Graham was soon off. Margot lay worried, staring at the pale furniture. At about three in the morning a tremendous bustle started in the road outside – the sound of lorries and cars passing almost incessantly. At daybreak she could discern the laden traffic going west.

The exodus of refugees had begun.

2

Next day Margot was on edge. The noise of the traffic went on all the morning. The proprietor was likely to burst into tears at any moment: France was upset, in a plight. Was the Boche to come again? Brokenly he described his grand-mother's experiences in the last occupation. When he began the tale for the third time since breakfast Graham went outside.

Margot followed him. They made their way through the groups of cars and people which had begun to collect and, in the scorching sunlight, went down to the river. Graham looked carefully for the tide.

'Can't do anything before seven this evening,' he said gaily.

Margot sounded out of control:

'Graham!'

He looked up quickly.

'What's the matter with you?'

She relaxed a little.

'Oh, you know,' she waved her arm in the direction of the village – the roar of the traffic could be heard plainly. 'All that business.'

'Well, it needn't affect us,' he said gently, 'we're neutrals. You ought to thank your lucky stars you're safe.'

'I know – but –' She was not convinced. She tore up a blade of grass and began to split it. 'It is pretty momentous though, isn't it?'

'What is?'

'Well – all of it.' Why didn't Graham see? She felt they were beginning not to understand each other.

'Oh, forget it,' he said irritably, 'I'm going fishing.'

'*Graham!*' Her eyes were wide open.

'Well, what about it?'

He waited. But she could not answer. She knew he was being quite consistent: he had never taken sides about the war. She had always known it and had never expected anything else.

'Well, what of it?'

He persisted, with dark, accusing eyes.

'Oh, I don't know.'

She went limp.

'Very well then,' he said and looked at the river, 'I'm off to find a place for tonight. There's a better reach higher up.'

He walked away quietly, his brown legs swinging through the uncut grass on the river bank, his shoulders swaying comfortably.

Margot watched him for about half a mile. Once or twice she nearly called after him, but stopped – and he did not look back. Her mind now worked quickly.

When all she could see of him was his bobbing dark head above the grass on the bank she turned and hurried back to the village. The hotel was now crowded with people eager to get something to eat. As she pushed by to reach the stairs she heard a man and a woman speaking English. They were standing just inside the café door, stuffing rolls and coffee down their mouths.

She went straight up to them.

'How are you getting away?'

The man answered quickly. 'By car to Bordeaux, if we're lucky. We hear there's a steamer there.'

'Will you take me with you?' she asked calmly. 'I have nearly fifteen pounds in French money, and I can find a British passport.'

The man and woman looked at one another. He raised his eyebrows, and she answered with a quick nod.

'Our car is only a two-seater,' said the man, 'But we can manage, I think. The point is – we're going *now*. You'll have to buck up.'

She gave them a rapid smile.

'All right.'

She ran upstairs to her room, took out a small suitcase from the bottom of the cupboard and packed it with a few essential things. Very carefully she wrote a short note for Graham and propped it against his photograph on the dressing-table. He regarded her from an angle, his pipe between his teeth, and his sports shirt open at the neck. A faintly cynical turn to the mouth struck her for the first time.

Above the noise of the traffic in the road outside she heard an impatient klaxon.

She took the suitcase and a warm coat and went quickly downstairs, past the hot and hungry travellers, into the road. The proprietor was doing his best to serve them all. When he saw Margot he called out, 'They say they are not more than thirty miles down the road. What will become of us?'

She had no time to answer even if she had wished, for the driver of the two-seater was signalling to her to hurry.

She pushed her way past a small cart piled high with a family's belongings and two bewildered children, and climbed onto the back of the car. In the heat and confusion she could not hear what the driver said to her. She just nodded. 'Hang on – that's all,' he repeated, 'We're going to make it as fast as this crowd'll let us.' She nodded again, but she had begun to feel numbed – as if it were happening to someone else.

The car started off, past the pony carts and wheelbarrows, the delivery vans and overcrowded saloons. Several had feather mattresses on their roofs, and on one a split wind-screen told its own story of machine-gun bullets.

They overtook a good deal of the traffic without difficulty

and soon had turned off down a short hill under some trees. It was cooler there and Margot's head began to clear.

'You all right?' called the driver.

'Yes, thanks,' she answered, clutching the back of the hood. At the bottom of the hill flowed the sun-dappled river. On the opposite bank stood a white village, surrounded by eucalyptus trees.

Somewhere upstream Graham was looking for a place to fish.

THE WOMAN NOVELIST

Madeleine finished dressing by the open window, looking down onto the garden. It was not yet seven, but she knew that the day was going to be hot, cloudless and unchanging, because of the vivid, almost unnatural green of the trees on the far edge of the dew-damp lawn. Nothing moved anywhere – except a blackbird, whose tail pitched like a see-saw as it alighted on a stone in the Flemish garden.

She paused, her hairbrush threaded into her dark, soft hair. The Flemish garden! It was bright yellow with charlock. Wykham should have tidied it – there were things that he had undertaken to do at weekends, and during his vacations from the law school – but he had not done so. There were, in fact, other things that he had not done.

He lay now, behind her in the room, in the bed nearest the wall. He still slept.

She felt suddenly despondent, although it was so early in the day. She often felt this nowadays, losing, as she did so, the glory of these summer mornings. Such small things, too, sent her skimming down. To keep the seven of them going – herself and Wykham, the three children, and the two old ladies, Wykham's mother and her mother, whose contributions

barely covered the rent – allowed no chance for anyone to slip up on their job. If anyone did that, she could not then carry on with hers, and it was by her work that they lived. Including Wykham. His state grant on leaving the Army barely covered his expenses in London, where he was studying for the Bar.

This last week he had been on vacation, and had spent it reading in his 'study', the old morning-room – was he reading law books or those green and white paperbacks which later she found imbedded in dust in the garbage-bin? – or visiting in the neighbourhood, which was remote enough to contain still a few of the orthodox, but ruined, and beginning to be faintly ridiculous, gentry, who made him feel – as he was handed a glass of brandy by a white-haired squire resembling his late father – that he counted somewhere in the world, that there was a place still for his 'type'. How he enjoyed this, Madeleine thought, softening. At those times, he would become vivid and alive, almost visibly becoming heavier – he was thin – and looking handsome in an old-fashioned way. She turned from the window and finished doing her hair. That was the sort of life Wykham ought always to live. He ought to have been born a hundred years before.

Her helplessness returned. She leaned one hand on the window-sill, her long, slim body twisted and drooping.

But then she thought of the book she was working on. Last week it had taken a new, interesting turn. It had come strongly to life. Her spirits rose. Those two and a half hours in the afternoon, when the children were at school, and the two old ladies, the mothers-in-law, were withdrawn, resting in their

bedrooms, were hers – hers for herself. Some of the joy of those hours now came to her. Her oval, nearly beautiful face – it had a small twist to it, so that the centre of her slightly pointed chin was not in line with the middle of her forehead – which, when first she had gone to the mirror, had been pinched and pale, was now filled out and glowing. She could carry on – the family was secure – if she were certain of those two and a half precious hours.

She went out onto the landing. It seemed very empty, and was bright, whitely bright, as if in some way it had been gutted by the night. She went into the children's rooms. Only the younger boy was still asleep. Robert and Jenny were already sitting up in bed, looking at books. She told them to get up and dress. She then went downstairs to the large, cool kitchen, let out the tortoiseshell cat, lit the Calor stove, and put on the kettle. The daylight grew stronger, less ethereal and exquisite; the ordinary day proceeded to arrive. A tractor began to climb, as if in pain, up the short hill, which rose beyond the edge of the garden.

Madeleine then thought of Beryl, her twenty-year-old help from two miles away down the valley. At half-past eight she would come, as fresh-cheeked as if she had collected dew on the way, on her bicycle, and with her fair hair crisp and shining, and scarcely out of place. Madeleine thought of her with a gratitude, deep and tender, like love. It was love. For how could she have managed without her? And she was always capable, willing, reliable. She seemed to like working out here at the White House – this old half-mansion among the untidy, farming acres.

As Madeleine made toast and fried the bacon, she heard her mother, Mrs Grinling, coming down the stairs – slowly, because of her rheumatics – to help. The tractor now turned at the bottom of the hill for a second ascent. What had the farmer planned for this morning, out there? Madeleine wondered, idly. It was too early for hay-making. Could it be ploughing? She scraped fat into the frying-pan and went and joined her mother in the dining-room. Mrs Grinling always laid the breakfast-table, but slowly and painfully, because of her stiff joints. The first child, Jenny, now came downstairs.

During the meal, the youngest, Timothy, spilt his milk; Jenny was gay and too talkative – she was taking anemones to her form-mistress, with whom she was in love. Robert ate his bacon contentedly. Thank goodness, Madeleine thought, they could all now dress themselves. But what, she wondered, would their rooms be like?

Afterwards, she and the old, white-haired lady watched them ride off on their bicycles down the long, white, empty road. There was little traffic in that part of the world, even in the small country town containing the school, so that they could be fairly trusted. The two women then returned to the house – Mrs Grinling to the dining-room for her last, private cup of tea and a brief look at her son-in-law's newspaper, and Madeleine to the kitchen. The warm May wind came soothingly, freshly, through the window – open – above the stone sink. She would have liked to do nothing more in the house all that day, but to have gone out into the garden and to have sat under the beech trees, thinking about, and working out, her novel. But she had still much to do, to get through.

Her next job was to prepare breakfast for the other old lady, Mrs Filmer, Wykham's mother.

She took it, with a letter, into the downstair bedroom, which had once been the drawing-room of the house, and had an ornate, moulded ceiling. Mrs Filmer had furnished it with large, late-Georgian furniture from the country house where she had been born. The old lady, her hair a faint blue-white, in neat, flat waves under an invisible hair-net, was sitting up in her mahogany bed, holding in readiness a silver paper-knife.

'Good morning, my dear', she said, brightly, 'I hope you slept well, and that the children have gone off safely.' She used the same words every morning.

'Yes, thank you, mama,' Madeleine answered, as usual.

She drew back the brocade curtains. On the path under the window a tricycle lay on its side over a crushed white, lidless shoe-box and some old tennis balls. She ought to have put them away last night, and not left it to the children. On this side of the house, the garden was even more neglected. Her despondency returned. If only Wykham would fulfil his promises! She leaned on the window-sill, and looked through the foliage of the trees, at the cornfield beyond. Why, she mused, had this large white house been built right out here, in the first place? Whose vision had started it all off? They had heard of it – to let cheap – through an ex-Army friend of Wykham's. And how enormous it was! The rooms had been designed for large house-parties, even balls: and yet it belonged to no especial period. She wondered how long they would be able to afford to live here. Her heaviness increased.

But once more she remembered her work, and the solace it brought her – as well as the money it earned. Again, she grew cheerful. Today she would work out in the conservatory, instead of, as was customary, in the dining-room. No one ever went there. She would be undisturbed. And the trees, having grown up round it, cooled it off. She would use the white painted bamboo table, and leave the door open so that, from time to time, she could look out onto the garden.

She turned back to her mother-in-law, whom she had almost forgotten.

The old lady smiled brilliantly, and said charmingly, but without sincerity – she was already returning to her letter – as she left the room: 'Now dear, you're to let me know if I can do anything to help you.'

Out in the sunny kitchen, Madeleine found Beryl putting on her snow-white overall. She was, as Madeleine had expected to see her, fresh, cheerful, neat – even elegant. She lived with her grandmother in a brick cottage beside the canal, in the nearby town.

'Good morning, Mrs Filmer.' Beryl's eyes were admiring and kind.

Together they cleared the breakfast-table – except for Wykham's things, which were left for him to enjoy peacefully. While on vacation, he never came down before ten. Beryl then started the washing-up, while Madeleine went upstairs to tidy the children's rooms. Passing Wykham's and her bedroom, she went in. He lay on his back, wide awake, staring at the ceiling. He was unusually good-looking, with a square jaw, deep-set blue eyes, and black, curly hair. He smiled at her, showing his

flawless teeth. She felt brighter. When he greeted her like this, she always felt warmed, soothed.

But then, through the window, as she turned her head, she saw once more the charlock choking the Flemish garden. She thought desperately: What a pity he has not cleared it, as he promised.

'I suppose I had better get up,' he muttered, feeling that she had accused him of lying in bed.

'And I must get on with my housework,' she said, flatly, going to the door.

He sat up and scratched his back with his thumbs, under his striped pyjama jacket. As she passed him she drew her hand lightly over his hair. He caught at her wrist, smiling.

She went to the children's rooms. As she had expected, they were in vivid, elemental disorder. The sun poured over them through the enormous square windows. Each child seemed to have left something of its own personality in all three rooms. Particularly Jenny. Madeleine could almost hear her high, eager and faintly irritating voice, as she went in. How unconcerned they all were by their parents' struggle to feed and educate them! She collected up their soiled underclothing. Tomorrow she and Beryl would have a big wash-day. She then ran the Ewbank over the threadbare, almost paper-thin Oriental rugs, which Wykham's mother had once given them.

When, finally, she went downstairs, Beryl was already preparing the lunch. Peeled potatoes lay, transparent-looking, in a bowl of water; cabbage leaves glistened under the tap. Beryl had also thoroughly 'done out' the dining-room, the hall, and the drawing-room – where Mrs Grinling now sat at the

desk, writing a letter. Old Mrs Filmer had not yet appeared. She did not usually arrive until lunchtime. Wykham must have gone already to his study.

Madeleine took a basket, and went out into the garden, to pick rhubarb, and a lettuce for salad. While out there she would transplant some of the young lettuces from the frame. She wished that Wykham could have been out there with her, that they could have had a little time alone together, as in the old days. But it would not have been right: she must not ask for it. She must do nothing to prevent him from one day getting to the Bar.

Wykham came and stood at the french window of the study, with his hands in his pockets. He found it almost impossible to concentrate these bright mornings. He wanted to go over again to see Colonel Clavering, at Place House. Would Madeleine mind; would the Colonel be in? He watched the white butterflies fluttering above the charlock in the Flemish garden. It was his mother who had called it the 'Flemish' garden. Very like her. Such big ideas still, when for so long she had possessed nothing more impressive than a downstairs bed-sitting-room.

He supposed, he thought idly, that he ought to have cleared out that charlock weeks ago. Now that he remembered, hadn't he promised Madeleine that he would do so?

2

At twelve, Madeleine returned to the house. Beryl was rolling the pastry for the rhubarb pie. Together, they built up the

lunch; fish for Mrs Filmer, salad for Mrs Grinling; 'solid' food for Wykham. The children took theirs at school. They worked silently and steadily. The kitchen felt peaceful, industrious. Once, Mrs Grinling came out to the kitchen for water for some flowers. Madeleine and she then laid the table for lunch.

When she heard the one o'clock time signal coming from the library Madeleine untied her apron, and went in there. Both the old ladies were there, trying to make conversation. At all other times of the day, they avoided each other. Wykham, in his new dark-grey flannel suit, was standing up reading aloud the label on a sherry bottle.

'I couldn't find the brown glasses, darling,' he said, to Madeleine, 'so I've used those.'

He pointed to a brandy glass on the spinet. With dismay, she saw that a ring of sherry had formed on the polished wood, showing white. Could it be removed? she wondered, anxiously.

But suddenly she decided that she would no longer mind so much about things like that. The most important thing was to get lunch over so that she could get to her novel. Was this progress: or was she growing old? She did not know. She sat down.

Wykham raised his glass. 'To all the Filmers,' he said, smiling.

Mrs Grinling tried, with a self-effacing smile, to feel included.

After lunch, Madeleine and Beryl washed up swiftly, for at half-past two, Beryl had to go. They then prepared the

children's tea, spreading it out on the great kitchen table. With every five minutes that passed, Madeleine's heart lifted: soon she would be working at her book.

At twenty-past two there were still a few small jobs to be done in the kitchen.

'I'll do them,' said Beryl. 'You go and get started, Mrs Filmer.'

Madeleine hesitated, but the determined understanding in the girl's clear eyes destroyed argument. She went to the dining-room, and collected her folder from the window-seat. An idea for the book's next sequence was already bubbling, like a fountain under pressure: clear images were waiting to be fixed on paper. But she must hurry. She was almost perspiring.

On her way through the hall, she met Wykham, standing, undecided, at the front door.

'Thought I might do a bit in the garden,' he said, vaguely. He hoped that she would make up his mind for him. He was still wondering whether or not to go over to Colonel Clavering. If he gardened, he would have to change his clothes.

'It's very hot,' she said, 'If you do, perhaps you ought to wear a hat.'

He half-barred her way, about to put his arm round her, but she would not stop. At this moment, she could give no more time to anyone.

She walked round the great, pale house – to the con-servatory, which looked out onto a deserted part of the garden. The door was jammed. She pushed it hard, and it ground open, scraping over the tiled floor. Inside, it was hot and airless. For thirty years nothing had been cultivated there and

the heating grills were rusted through. Entering, she felt as if she had stepped into another, earlier time.

She pulled the bamboo table up to the open door, so that, while working, she could feel the summer air on her bare arms. She sat down swiftly, and opened out her folder.

3

Wykham decided, in the end, to clear the Flemish garden. He turned up his trousers at the ankles. They'd be all right like that, surely! He then went out to the garage, to fetch a fork. If only he'd tackled the job a fortnight ago, when the ground was softer. Today, he'd probably break the fork.

The garage was crammed. Under a dust-sheet was a car, wheel-less, blocked-up. He had bought it with the idea of one day making it go. On all sides were garden tools and children's toys. He had to climb over a pile of tomato boxes, to get at the fork.

He then saw Beryl's bicycle against the wall. Like herself, it was gleaming, bright, new, and he felt a sudden surge of admiration, envy, for her, which came to him now frequently, when he saw her. Whatever she did, she did so well. Success for her seemed certain. He sought for the fork in a group of rusted garden tools.

Just after half-past two, Beryl came out. She had folded up her white overall to put in the bicycle basket. She did not see Wykham deep in the garage, watching her. He kept very still. How fresh and clean she is, he thought. More like a smart dentist's assistant, than a house-help.

He half-lent against the covered car, to watch her better. Without meaning to, he moved a bucket.

She started.

'I didn't know you were there, sir.'

Without speaking, still watching her, he came forward, climbing slowly over the tomato boxes. Again he was thinking: How fresh she is.

She stood, seeing his approach, as if transfixed.

He was now very near her. Suddenly, thoughtlessly, he leaned forward and gently took hold of her wrist. She was surprised, looking at him in the eyes. Slowly and deliberately, he bent and kissed her on the mouth.

She stepped back, her blue eyes steady and reproving.

'No, Mr Filmer,' she said. 'Not that. I'm not here for that. I'm here to help Mrs Filmer.'

He looked down, foolishly.

'You ought not to do that, you know,' she went on, as if speaking to a child.

He now spoke quickly: 'I'm extremely sorry. I can't think what came over me.'

'That's all right then,' she answered, stern, still reproving.

Under his thick, rather pale skin he looked hot, awkward. He helped her wheel her bicycle out of the garage. He watched her get up on it.

'Goodbye, sir'.

'Goodbye, Beryl,' he said.

She rode out into the lane.

He turned back nervously, to get the fork.

He was suddenly deeply worried. Supposing that Beryl,

after this, gave notice? What, then, would happen to them? Madeleine depended on Beryl – or else she could not write – and the rest of them, including himself, depended on Madeleine, and Madeleine's writing. He must do nothing, must never do anything that might make Beryl not want to come to the house. He ought to have thought of this before.

And when, he wondered, would he be able to earn enough to support this family of his and Madeleine's? Fear cut through him. He felt small, young, doomed. During the war he had felt like this sometimes.

He searched among the tools. He had better hurry up and clear the charlock from the Flemish garden.

4

On the far side of the house, everything was deeply still; the conservatory was enfolded by silence. In that detached, blazing hour after lunch even the birds were withdrawn, not moving, or visible, and the tractor which, all morning, had droned on the hill was now quiet.

Madeleine looked at her manuscript. This next section was going to be the most difficult and involved, and the most significant. How would her two central characters – the man and the woman – come together again? If she could get this next part to go right, the rest would follow. Surely she could do it; surely she had the power? The answer was very near the surface of her mind. She must let her mind go free, so that she could pick it up.

She looked up, letting her gaze wander out on the garden.

Her thoughts then left the book and she unexpectedly thought of Wykham and Beryl. She believed that Wykham liked Beryl. He often grew quiet when he joined them in the kitchen, and stood, staring at her, his blue eyes dense and dark. She knew his tendency to admire twenty-year-olds, she thought wryly. Was this likely to grow less, or to develop? she wondered. But out here, she was without anxiety about the idea. She could review it calmly. Yet what would happen if Wykham were to make a pass at Beryl? What would Beryl do? She felt then, almost instantly, as she looked down at the white sheet of paper in front of her, that she had such trust in Beryl, and the girl's common-sense – that Beryl, apart from her loyalty to her, Madeleine, had some plan in life which would not be deflected by the passing advances of the husband of her employer – that she could not feel anxious about this. It was more likely that Beryl would leave, if Wykham got fresh. She was only out here because she liked it, and liked working for Madeleine. But if Beryl were no longer here to help her, the fat would be on the fire. Then her troubles would really start. For it was almost impossible to get help so far out. What would she do? For a moment, she felt helpless, lost, almost trembling. She wondered how she would be able to go on with her book.

And for all she knew, Wykham might at this very moment be making those passes at Beryl. They were alone on that side of the house. She had left him, half-amorous, at the door. What a risk she had taken!

But she looked again at her work, at the open folder and the white page, and her old strength came back. She always had this – to earn money, to keep the family going. Somehow

they would survive by it, whatever happened. Even if Wykham did not get to the Bar for years. Even if Beryl went away. She could cope – if she had this.

She heard then a bee humming against the glass in the depths of the conservatory, and got up to lift it in her handkerchief, and let it go free through the door. It flew off, vivid with relief. She returned to her bamboo chair, and sat down – its creaking was the only sound in the silence. She knew now how to go on; how to link up her characters. Yes, this was right. Such and such would follow; and so on. She took up her pen and began to write swiftly, without pausing.

A beam of sunlight, striking through a break in the clouded glass above her head, struck across the white page.

CROSSING THE ATLANTIC

1

In the largest cabin of the *Florian*, in which one could scarcely stick one's elbows out, Macnab sat, with his plimsolled feet on the flap table.

'Lone Atlantic Crossing on Home-made Cutter', he read savagely. 'At this moment a neat 40 ft cutter is lying in the harbour. It was designed, built, and is to be sailed across the Atlantic by one man: Charles Macnab, aged thirty-eight, one time solicitor's clerk, stoker on ocean liner, and dish-washer. He plans to start his trip tomorrow, the 13th, despite the associations of the date, and to reach New York in three months' time. The boat is amply stocked with provisions. When I asked the boat-builder, captain and crew rolled into one, what made him contemplate the trip, he answered: "I plan on getting a rest from civilisation for a while."'

Footsteps rang on the deck above and a moment later the writer of the article – a man named Protheroe – thrust his bland face through the hatch:

'Have you finished your supper?'

Macnab got to his feet. He was short, with a large head. 'I thought I told you I didn't want publicity,' he stormed.

Unabashed, Protheroe climbed down into the cabin. 'How about farewells at the Blue Peter?'

Macnab shook his head. 'At five-thirty, I've to be away on the morning tide.'

Protheroe sat on the edge of the bunk.

'Very well, we'll drink here.'

Macnab went ungraciously to the locker and brought out brandy. After that it was a simple matter to get him to the Blue Peter at the end of the quay.

Some fishermen and a yachtsman in a peaked cap greeted them cheerfully as they entered. 'So you're off at last,' said an old salt. 'Glad I'm not in your boots.' The yachtsman clapped him on the back. 'Didn't know until I read my *Western Argus* that you loathed the sight of us.'

Macnab was at once surrounded by a small crowd.

It is here that the young woman comes into the tale. She was wearing a striped jersey and blue linen slacks, and carried a cigarette holder. Leaving her table she came over to Protheroe and laid a hand on his arm (her nails were crimson and faintly stained with nicotine).

'You've got a celebrity here. Who is it?'

'He's sailing the Atlantic alone in the morning.'

Her eyes widened.

'The little fellow in the middle!' she said incredulously. 'Introduce me, will you?'

Protheroe tapped Macnab's shoulder. He turned round sharply. The young woman put out her hand. 'How do you do. I'm Cora Nathan,' she said, looking down at him. 'I hear you're off to the States in the morning. I'm sailing from

Plymouth in a week's time. Hadn't we better have a drink
on it?'

In silence Macnab ordered the drinks and paid for them.

'Is that the name of your boat?' she asked, pointing to the
word 'Florian' on the front of his jersey.

He nodded. 'Who are you?'

'I'm a journalist in a way,' she explained with a smile. 'I've
reported flower shows until I'm crazy.'

He ordered more drinks. After she had deftly exchanged
their glasses she had very nearly made Macnab thaw.

'You know,' he said presently, 'I can't make out why a girl
like you isn't married.'

'I was once,' she answered brightly.

A few moments later she looked pensively into her glass
and then at him.

'Why don't you take someone with you on this trip?'

'Because I prefer my own company.'

'How about when you're bored?'

'My boat isn't big enough to lose someone on.'

'It is – if the "someone" knew when to make herself
scarce.'

He shook his head. 'No such person exists.'

'Why not try it?' she said archly. 'Me, for example.'

He looked at her incredulously. 'You'd have to peel potatoes
and stitch sails till your fingers hurt.'

She answered feverishly: 'I'd do that – I'd do anything
to make a name crossing the Atlantic with you. Think what
a welcome we'd get in New York' – she was very excited – 'We
could get that reporter man to cable we were coming.'

Panic flashed in Macnab's eyes. 'Now then – not so fast. I didn't say you could.'

He turned to finish his glass and Cora hastily drew Protheroe to one side. 'I've got a story for you,' she said in an undertone.

Protheroe inclined his head.

'I'm going with Macnab!'

His jaw dropped.

'You don't say!'

She nodded quickly. 'Here are my particulars: I'm twenty-nine; I'm an – an international journalist; I've seen Hitler at Nüremberg, and I've written a novel.'

2

At ten-past ten the Blue Peter closed. Cora accompanied Macnab back to the boat. By now she was stone sober and he was beginning to stumble. As she climbed after him into the cabin he made a clumsy effort to put his arm round her.

'No thanks, Charles,' she said firmly, with one hand on the word 'Florian'. 'Let me see the boat first.'

He opened a door into a minute cabin astern. 'That's where I sleep.' He swung his arm round toward the fo'c'sle. 'And that's where I cook.'

He sat down heavily on the bunk in the centre cabin. 'Why don't you sit down?'

'I haven't finished looking at the boat,' she answered airily.

She went aft and struck a match. Macnab's sleeping quarters were extremely neat. 'This'll do me fine,' she thought. 'Thank goodness I'm a good sailor.'

When she came back Macnab had dozed off.

'I hope he doesn't snore,' she thought, 'I never could get on with men who snore.'

She returned to the minute cabin in the stern and fixed the door with her shoe. Without troubling to undress she climbed onto the bunk and was soon fast asleep.

3

At seven-thirty the *Florian* sailed past the harbour-master's office, going down river. They had very nearly lost the tide through argument. Cora was below, making herself a cup of tea, her hair disordered because Macnab would not lend her his comb.

In an hour's time they were in the open sea: the little boat pitching irritably among the fast-flowing waves. As Cora came on deck Macnab was taking in the topsail, his brow black with rage.

'Don't be cross,' she gaily chided him. 'In a day or two you'll be glad you've got me with you.'

He made no reply.

The houses on the coast were no larger than thimbles. Two gulls which had followed them with acquisitive eyes now flew off at the approach of a liner.

Towards noon Cora went below and began a diary in an exercise book Macnab had bought for navigation. It kept her busy for quite a while, during which time she smoked innumerable cigarettes.

4

At five o'clock they were somewhere off Land's End, tacking against a head wind. The sea was dark blue.

Macnab had spent the whole day on deck, taking no notice of Cora when she came up for air. At six he felt hungry, and after taking a long look at the sea he fixed the tiller and went below.

Cora was full-length on the bunk with *The Navigation of Currents and their Courses* propped open on her chest.

He looked about sullenly, swaying with the boat.

'Have you got lunch ready?'

His tone would have frightened most people.

'As you were so unsociable I thought you didn't want any,' she answered sleepily, throwing down the book. 'Why haven't you anything more readable than this?'

'I didn't expect gate-crashers.'

He went into the tiny galley. The unwashed breakfast things were stacked beside the Primus.

'Why isn't the washing-up done?' he thundered.

She sat up slowly. 'Where's the hurry? If we're going to be like this for weeks I can do it later.'

He returned to the cabin, his eyes flashing.

'This is my boat – and if I want the washing-up done, it'll be done. Do you see? I don't want you on board, but since you're here you'll obey orders.'

She rose, went to the kitchen and lit the Primus. Fifteen minutes later he heard the clink of washing-up. His darkened brows did not alter as he munched a ham sandwich that he had to make himself.

By nine o'clock Cora was in her bunk. The bobbing of the boat had given her a 'head', but the flapping of the water against the hull soon sent her off to sleep.

After Macnab had entered up the log he turned down the swinging lamp and went above to get their position. Lighthouses flashed on either horizon as the *Florian* kept on her way busily.

He took the tiller lovingly in his horny hand. 'A bit of all right,' he murmured. 'Looks, too, as if the weather'll hold.'

'Damn that woman below.'

5

Cora had been certain that, in a day or two, they would be on the best of terms. After all, every man is human and few like to be in solitary confinement in the middle of the ocean for long. The time would come when, after their supper of fried bacon and ship's biscuits, she would entertain him with anecdotes from her varied life.

But the expected did not occur: Macnab's anger remained. He spent most of his time on deck, and slept so little that Cora wondered at his energy. When he came below it was only to collect a sandwich and a cup of coffee and to go on deck again. He refused to forgive her.

Quite soon Cora began to feel heartily bored. To have shared the adventure with Macnab would have made up for its loneliness, but this was not to be. After a week at sea, in which they made a considerable distance, she had read all the ship's literature and, after tidying the cabin and manicuring her

hands, she had very little to do but sleep. Her diary no longer allured her since all she could now muster were such sentences as: 'A gull appeared from nowhere and followed us a long way before flying off, having had nothing to eat.'

In the end she began to follow Macnab about.

'I don't mind if you keep out of my way,' he rounded on her when she inquired timidly after knots and splices. 'Then I'll try and pretend you're not on board.'

But he found this difficult because she used a special kind of perfume: when he went below from the airy Atlantic he entered an alien world. If the weather allowed he opened the portholes.

'Why the hell don't you give up that scent!' he growled.

In the evenings the cabin was filled with cigarette smoke.

When they were two weeks at sea she had a brainwave. If she wrote her life in great detail she calculated that she would be occupied until the end of the trip. It might even interest Macnab. She found a roll of kitchen paper, spread it on the table and kept it in place with two tins of baked beans.

For some days Macnab had the deck to himself. With his hand on the tiller and the spray in his face he very nearly forgot all about her.

They had yet to run into bad weather.

6

This happened a thousand miles from land.

After battening down the hatch and covering the skylights with canvas Macnab donned an oilskin and sat out all day and

all night. When the dawn broke through raging yellow clouds he reefed down, set the stormsail, and rocked down the ladder to try and make some tea.

Cora lay strapped to her bunk with her eyes tight shut, trying to remember the names of the streets in South Kensington.

At four o'clock the storm increased, and had yet a long way to go. Early on the following morning Macnab hove to and went below to snatch a little sleep – while the *Florian* pitched dangerously amid the mountainous waves. He was too fagged out to care.

7

On the third day the bowsprit snapped in two and, in a tangle of rigging, seemed about to beat a hole in the hull.

Macnab scrambled below. Cora was strapped to her bunk with an oilskin over her head.

'Look here,' he rapped out, his mouth white with brine, 'I've a hell of a risky job to tackle and you've got to help me.'

She turned back the oilskin and looked out, her eyes large with fear.

'But I don't know anything about boats. Really I don't.'

'Well – now's your chance to learn.'

'But I – I haven't been on deck for a week. Supposing I go overboard?'

Just then the broken bowsprit beat an ominous tattoo outside.

'For God's sake – get on these oilskins and join me on deck as soon as you can.'

He opened the hatch on a breaking wave. Cora thought the *Florian* was about to capsize. The boat heeled right over and sprang back with a whine of wind and water.

Her heart failed her. 'I can't do it. I can't.' Gripping the side of the bunk she cried out hopelessly: 'Oh, when *shall* we get to America!'

The light was going. The waves which screeched down on them were capped with turrets of foam. From the crest of one of them Macnab saw the broken horizon and wads of black cloud. If things got worse it would be the end of the *Florian*. He looked up with moist eyes at the swinging mast. 'I shall go down with my boat,' he thought.

Aloud he said: 'That woman'll be here in a jiffy.'

But Cora did not come, and alone Macnab repaired the bowsprit.

At three in the morning the storm reached its climax. Macnab, at the tiller, was drenched to the skin. At six o'clock, in a mountainous sea with broken waves and scudding clouds, he detected a slackening of the wind. At lunch-time a white bird appeared on the water. He hove to and went below.

Cora, in silence, made him a peanut butter sandwich and a cup of tea. There was a loaded silence between them. She could not meet his eyes, and he would not look at her.

All at once the sea calmed. Except for a few streaky clouds the sky was blue. Macnab slept for a day and a half.

When he awoke Cora had finished her autobiography, and was biting her nails.

'How far are we from America?' she asked brightly.

From then on Macnab appeared not to see her. Yet whenever he came into the cabin his presence was so disagreeable that she either retired to her cabin or went on deck.

They now ran into semi-tropical weather with very little wind. Cora took blankets and a pillow and slept all day in the sun.

Once she tried to make conversation with Macnab, who now had a beard five inches long. He ignored her.

'All right,' she said airily, 'don't talk if you don't want to. Before long we'll be in New York.'

Macnab himself was not as unaware of her presence as he made out. He thought about her a great deal – particularly when she brushed against him on her way to the foredeck to lie down. He would go below into the gloom, to pore over his maps and wind-charts in private. But even there he could not get away from the thought of her: in a saucer on the table lay stub ends of cigarettes, stained with lipstick, and her odour lingered with the brine.

One evening as she was making tea he gripped the table in a spasm of rage and, half-rising, snarled at her back:

'You little bitch!'

She swung about quickly.

'Nearly sent this boat to the bottom, you did,' he said, with a frightful glare.

Cora was nervous. She turned to the tea-pot and filled it quickly. At any moment she expected him to lay hands on her – but when she looked round he was again seated at the table, his pipe alight, working out their position.

Her hands trembled as she drank her tea.

9

The next week Cora found boring. The sun went in; the cabins were soon cleaned. Macnab went about in a smouldering rage, his beard longer, his hands horny and yellow.

'He's hardly an Adonis,' she thought, once more reading *The Navigation of Currents and their Courses*, this time with the map open.

When they were ten days off New York she saw a liner go by, followed by a string of gulls. Wild with excitement she cleaned her shoes and brushed her slacks. She longed for a hair-set. Clamouring newspaper men would meet them on the quay; thenceforward, it would be a simple matter to get a job over there. She supposed Macnab would go back the way he had come. He'd be happy alone. Probably he'd run into another storm – worse than the one they'd weathered. In which case the *Florian* might go down. She rather hoped it would.

10

But Macnab did not feel that to arrive in New York would solve his troubles. During the long night watches, when the masthead swung to right and to left across the stars, his anger grew to ominous proportions. He went off his feed. He went below only to get a few hours' uneasy sleep and to nibble a ship's biscuit. He no longer enjoyed his pipe, and seemed sallow and thin.

It was when they were three days off New York and a southerly wind blew over a choppy grey sea that Macnab

decided to act. His appetite and his colour instantly returned. If Cora had thought more about him she might have felt uneasy at the change.

The *Florian* toppled so much from side to side when he went to examine the slope of the deck and the proximity of such things as the shortened bowsprit and the rigging, that he could scarcely stand. At one place someone slipping would slide into the sea without more ado. He went through the motion of throwing away the slops. Perfect, he thought. He looked round: the green ocean swirled past. Not a ship, not an iceberg, to be seen.

He fetched a bar of soap and rubbed the deck until it gleamed with a blue film, then he went below and ordered Cora to empty the potato peelings.

'Why do it now?' she asked.

'They've been there for an hour,' he answered, as if he had something in his throat. 'And be careful you don't foul the mainsail.'

She decided not to argue. Taking the pail she swung slowly up the ladder.

'Any more orders?' she mocked.

'Yes,' he hissed. 'Go and drown yourself,' and cursed himself for nearly giving the show away.

She did as she was told. On deck she looked at the sky and wondered why she had spent so long in the fuggy cabin. Before long they would be in New York. She took the pail and went to the side.

As Macnab had hoped, the boat tipped first one way and then the other. As it came back her foot slipped on the soapy

deck and the pail went flying overboard. She followed. Below, Macnab heard the thud. His eyes and mouth shut tight. The end, thank God!

But he had not foreseen that Cora was lightly built and that her nails were long. As she went she dug her fingers into the deck and broke her fall. From there she reached out and somehow grasped the rigging. In the next second her head was under water. The *Florian* tipped again, and she found herself spreadeagled on the hull with the sea beneath her. She clambered up but was again flung back as the boat tipped over. She choked and gurgled, and cried out.

In the end she rescued herself.

When she had recovered sufficiently she went below. Macnab seemed surprised to see her; he even made her a cup of tea. She collapsed on the bunk in her drenched clothes.

Eventually she spoke: 'That deck seemed awfully slippery. I'm – I'm – I'm afraid I lost the pail.'

Macnab grabbed his cap and went on deck. He was a long time swabbing it down, after which the *Florian* changed tack.

1 1

Two days later they sighted a pink lightship on a green desert of sea. As they sailed by, about a mile off a Yankee flag flew up in greeting. Cora waved ecstatically.

An hour later an aeroplane approached, scouring the sea. Finally it reached the *Florian*, dipped low and roared over them. Some heads were thrust out and several arms waved.

'Look, Charles. Look,' Cora cried, 'especially for us!'

Macnab, biting his lips, said nothing.

The elephantine monoplane roared homeward. It was going to turn out exactly as Cora had hoped.

12

The next day they ran before the wind down Long Island Sound. At four-thirty they beached.

A hook-nosed official ran down to meet them, followed by a group of bright-eyed newspaper men with cameras and felt hats.

'I've been waiting for you for a month,' he said, clapping Macnab on the shoulder, and putting his arm round Cora's waist. 'But I must say I never thought you'd make it.'

Macnab lowered his head, and Cora stabbed her toe into the sand.

The journalists began to jostle them.

'What do you think now you're here?'

'Who did the washing-up?'

'Who mended the sails?'

'What do you think of Hitler?'

One, a little larger than the rest, wearing his hat on the back of his head, put his face between Cora's and Macnab's.

'I'm Golding, of the *Moon*. But before I get a story out of you I'd like you to stand back on the ship.'

Cora climbed on to the *Florian* with alacrity, followed slowly by Macnab.

Golding fixed his camera with three clicks, and all the other cameras did the same. Everyone was smiling except Macnab.

'Stand a little closer, please,' Golding asked politely.

Cora edged against Macnab. Where they stood the deck was unusually clean.

'Now put your arms round each other,' said another voice with another camera.

Cora put her arm round Macnab's waist. Like a firing squad the camera eyes blinked away at them.

'Now from another angle,' called someone else.

Finally, Golding took compassion on them.

'These folks are just about knocked out, I guess. How about giving them a let-down?'

Macnab sat on the hatch while everyone started lighting cigarettes and asking them questions, to which Cora cheerfully replied.

'Say, Macnab, I've had eyestrain looking for you,' said Golding, putting his hands in his pockets and rocking back and forth on his feet. 'I thought you'd gone to feed the sharks.'

'I can't understand,' said Macnab slowly, 'how you knew we were coming. I never told anyone.'

'A friend of yours cabled me – a guy called Protheroe.'

The big man leaned forward confidentially and winked broadly.

'And don't you worry, sailor. Everything's OK. I've carried out his instructions to the letter' – he patted his breast pocket – 'I've got the licence here. You can be married tomorrow at seven. Or earlier – tonight, if you wish. Anyway – just as soon as you want to. It's all fixed.'

He laid a puffy hand on Macnab's shoulder.

'But you've got to let me be the best man.'

THE COUPLE FROM LONDON

I was polishing the glasses when the lady and gentleman came into the bar. I turned to Mabel, she's the larger and more florid of us two, and I remember saying: 'He's a pale one.'

And so he was. There were great dark rings under his eyes, and his lips were thin and blue. He was dressed in a grey suit, very well cut, and his shoes were light brown and highly polished. Anyone could see he was a gentleman. He ordered a whiskey and soda for himself and a glass of port for the lady.

I liked the look of her at once. She was much younger than he was, fair and a little pathetic. She seemed very fond of him, standing by him all the time, saying: 'Ralph' this and 'Ralph' that.

The proprietor fetched up two chairs for them and asked them to sit down. He evidently thought the gentleman looked frail. Mabel and I exchanged glances. Poor lady! I thought. How awful to have an ailing husband.

They talked quietly enough while I went on with my work. I couldn't hear what they were saying though Mabel did remember hearing the gentleman say something about 'wishing to God people would mind their own business.' But that didn't help us solve the matter afterwards.

They had been sitting in the bar for well over an hour when the gentleman asked the proprietor if there was good fishing in the neighbourhood.

'What do you say to staying here a day or two?' he asked the lady, and smiled ever so sweetly at her. It was very touching to see how he doted on her.

She smiled back at him.

'I think it would be lovely, Ralph,' she answered.

They seemed very much in love with each other. I remember it struck me as queer because they didn't look as if they were newly-weds.

We served them up a cold lunch in the parlour. Afterwards I got the boy to run their bags up to No. 5, a nice double room overlooking the river, while the gentleman drove his car into the stables.

When it came to signing the visitors' book there was some slight trouble. The lady didn't want to do it.

'It's not me, ma'am,' the boss said. 'But the police. We're tied by regulations in this country, and no mistake.'

'You may as well sign, dear,' the gentleman said.

I looked in the book afterwards and read:

'Ralph Tylden, London,'

Juliet Tylden, London.'

Juliet, I thought. Looks like a Juliet, all innocent and loving.

In the afternoon they went for a long walk down the river. I watched them set off, her arm in his, the gentleman's thin back bent over towards her, very affectionate. When they got to the bridge he had a good look over, while she wandered off.

Looked to me as if she didn't care much for fishing, I thought. But he soon caught up with her.

'Can't make that couple out,' I said to Mabel, over our tea. She was busy with the *Daily Mail* and didn't want to talk, so I took up my knitting.

That evening Mabel was in the bar and I was sent off to serve the couple from London. They were tired after their long walk and ate everything I put in front of them. I heard Mrs Tylden tell him not to eat so quickly several times, but he seemed preoccupied. She looked at him anxiously once or twice. He seemed not to notice her half the time, just sat there eating, with his eyes glued to his plate. I don't think they had had a row or anything. It was just that there was something on his mind.

I made a nice fire up for them in the lounge. They went there afterwards and had a cup of coffee. He took out a very expensive cigar: everything he did showed that he was a man of means.

'Thank you very much,' he said, looking over the back of his armchair. 'My wife and I do not require anything else. We'll ring for you if necessary.'

'Thank you, sir,' I answered.

I must say my heart was touched by them. I went into the kitchen and filled them two hot-water bottles. Next, I went upstairs and turned their bed back, drew the curtains, emptied the wastepaper basket and burnt the contents in the fireplace. They had thrown away a lot of old letters.

'Sleep well, and bless you,' I said, patting the pillows.

I felt a bit anxious when I thought how pale the gentleman

looked. Lucky for him he had such a loving wife, I said to myself.

They went up about nine-thirty, and I heard him splashing about for a long time in the bathroom.

After that I helped Mabel out in the bar. There had been a market in the town that day and we were kept busy until after eleven. As I came to bed I noticed that the visitors' room was in darkness, for there was no light under the door. The night was dark and quiet, with no wind. I remember I lay awake a long time, and my thoughts would keep coming back to those two.

2

Next morning she came down to breakfast alone. As I came into the parlour the sun struck across the breakfast things and I saw her standing by the window. She had her back to me and there was something about her that I didn't like. As I jangled the tray on the table she swung round, as if she had not heard me come in. She was very pale, and her eyes were big, as if she had not slept.

'Oh, it's you,' she said.

And who else, I thought, would you expect at this time of the morning?

Though I didn't like the look of her, I thought I'd better keep quiet. She stood, fixed in the window, staring at me all the time I laid the cloth. Something's up, I said to myself. I could feel how she was desperate.

At last I said: 'It's going to be a lovely day.'

'A lovely day!' she repeated, as if she did not quite understand. 'Oh, yes . . . yes, a lovely day.' She turned then and looked out of the window. The sun was shining on the willows and everything looked lovely.

'Something's up,' I said to Mabel in the kitchen, jerking my head in the direction of the parlour.

When I returned with the grapefruit and the bacon and eggs and laid them on the table, she was still looking out of the window. In the end, seeing she wasn't going to move until she was made to, I said:

'Breakfast's ready, ma'am.'

She started. Jumpy, and no mistake, I thought.

'Oh, thank you,' she said. 'Thank you, but . . .' looking over the table. 'But my husband is ill this morning, and will not be down to breakfast.'

So that was it, I thought.

'Then I'll get a tray and take it up to him,' I made to go into the kitchen, but she stopped me.

'No . . . no, please don't,' she said. 'He's not well enough to . . . to eat. I think it would be better . . . better if he lay sleeping for a little while. He had a very bad night.'

'Very well, ma'am,' I answered. 'Just as you say.'

I took the second plate of bacon and eggs back into the kitchen and had them myself while Mabel was sweeping out the bar.

I wondered what could be the trouble with the gentleman. She certainly kept very quiet in there over her breakfast. Presently I heard her come out and go upstairs. She walked about a little on the landing before going into the bedroom, as

if making up her mind. When I went in to clear the breakfast things, I found she'd hardly eaten anything at all, except drink a cup of tea. I gave the bacon to the dog.

'Looks as if the gentleman was very poorly,' I said to our boss, when he came in with the sawdust. 'I don't like the look of the lady.'

'Just keep an eye on her,' he said. 'And find out if there's anything we can do.'

I hung about after that between the kitchen and the parlour, and took advantage of it to clean out the hall. Presently she came downstairs. She was dressed to go out in her hat and coat, and had her handbag and gloves.

'You're there. Good,' she said. 'I hoped you would be.' She came towards me and took my arm. I laid the broom against the wall and went with her into the parlour. I must say I didn't like the look on her face.

'I'm going out now,' she said. 'To fetch a doctor.'

'We can telephone for one,' I offered.

She was a little taken aback.

'Oh. Well, you see . . . he's not as bad as all that. I mean . . . I must go into town and buy special medicines for him. I know just what to get.'

'Yes, ma'am,' I said.

'But I want you to promise me, please, that you won't disturb him until I get back. He's sleeping now, and it's the best thing for him. But he's a very poor sleeper, and the least sound will wake him!'

She had opened her handbag and brought out a note-case. She drew out ten shillings.

'As it is so important that he should lie quietly, would you undertake to see that he does?' She offered me the money.

I put both hands behind my back, and shook my head.

'Really no, ma'am, thank you all the same. It'd be a pleasure to do as you say.'

She tried hard to get me to take the money, but I wouldn't. It was because I liked her. I wish now that I had. At least somebody would have got something out of it.

At last she said: 'Very well, then. And thank you very much. I'm sure I can rely on you.'

As she was getting the car out, I asked her what time she would be back.

'For lunch,' she answered.

I watched the car drive out of sight. That was the last we saw or heard of her.

When lunch-time came and she never turned up, the proprietor began to get worried.

'Suppose she's had an accident?' he said.

'She'd have rung up.'

'What about the gentleman?'

'She said he wasn't to be disturbed until she came back,' I said quickly.

'Give her another hour, then.'

At four o'clock we were all worried. Mabel and I kept looking at each other, wondering. When we made our tea, I took out an extra cup for the gentleman and cut two thin slices of bread and butter. 'Never too ill for that,' I said to Mabel. 'Poor fellow! And the bed not made and everything. Wonder what she's up to.'

I went upstairs with the tray, and knocked on the door. As I got no answer, I opened it very carefully, and peeped in. He was lying on his back and his head showed up against the pillow. By this time the sun had gone round to the back of the house, and the room was quite dark, since the blinds were drawn.

I went over softly and said, as gently as I could:

'Here's a cup of tea for you, sir.'

But I needn't have bothered, because he was dead.

I nearly dropped the tray when I realised, but I'm not much given to nerves, and I've seen a bit of death already. Instead, I laid it down and had a better look. Dead he was, and he was a nasty colour. I touched him to see if he was warm, but he was stone cold. And stiff, by the look of things.

I went down to get the proprietor. He rang for a doctor. We all had to drink a glass of brandy in the bar.

'He must have been dead a long time,' I said. 'I wonder if she knows?'

'I wonder if she did him in,' said Mabel.

'We'll know that soon,' said the proprietor.

The doctor was not long in coming. He was in the bed-room for some time.

'Looks to me like a simple case of heart,' he said down-stairs. 'But I shall have to have a *post mortem*. Meanwhile the widow must be notified.'

Of course the police had to be called in. They asked a lot of questions of Mabel and me, and then began other enquiries. We heard in a few days that they'd traced the gentleman's home and all about him, but he hadn't got a wife. She had

died seven years before. He lived in a club in London, and had a little girl at school in the country. As for the lady, nobody knew who she was; and they never did find out. She vanished right away; and that was the end of her.

We often talk about them, Mabel and I, wondering what it was all about and what really happened. At the inquest it came out he died of heart failure, pure and simple, and nothing else, though Mabel is inclined to think the doctor was wrong and he'd really been poisoned.

But this I never agree with. When I think of that Juliet, I just can't believe she would ever do a thing like that. The night they spent with us must have been terrible for her. The doctor said he'd been dead for eighteen hours. So he must have died soon after they went to bed, and she must have been too scared of being found out or something to come and tell us.

I must say, I wouldn't relish sleeping with a corpse.

MRS LUMLEY

Is this the house where Mrs Lumley lived? thought Angela, following the house-agent into the empty hall. If so, I shan't take it. The sun beat through the windows of the bare drawing-room, half visible beyond the door at the end. Was it here, or next door? she asked herself. Her mother had once brought her to tea with Mrs Lumley, but it was so long ago – and she could not remember. Swansea porcelain had held their tea and cakes. The cakes had been good – but they had stuck in Angela's throat because she had not liked Mrs Lumley. Children were strange creatures! She had disliked her without reason it seemed, and yet today, when houses were scarce and her need for one imperative, she could not take this house if Mrs Lumley had once lived in it.

The agent spoke. 'It's a charming house. Old – but with all modern conveniences. You can see it's in excellent condition.'

Here was the opportunity: 'Did – did a Mrs Lumley live here once?'

The agent – he was quite young, with sandy hair and freckles – was loath to disappoint her. 'That I can't say, madam. I'm new to the town. But our Mr Morgan, in the office, could tell you.'

They went into the dining-room which overlooked the neat public gardens. It seemed to be the same house – and yet the row was identical. She looked about: on the black marble mantelpiece her memory provided Mrs Lumley's silent gold clock; the Chelsea figures; a photograph of Dr Lumley, looking very old-fashioned; a sepia one of her son, James – at that time a cadet at Dartmouth. Also, but she could not remember where, there had been a photograph of Mrs Lumley. This was clearer in her mind than was Mrs Lumley herself: a dark woman wearing – yes! – a cameo brooch. Why then, since the photograph was pleasant – even charming – had Mrs Lumley left a memory that was distasteful?

As they went up the stairs their footsteps made the house ring like a box; Angela tried again to recapture the tea party and in particular, Mrs Lumley. What made her dislike her? She was the mother of a pleasant-looking boy; she had surrounded herself with nice things; she made delicious cakes. Perhaps when I get to the drawing-room I shall remember, she thought, shaking herself out of uncertainty and looking about.

The wallpapers were in good condition, although damp had stained the chief bedroom. They stood there for a few moments looking down into the public gardens. A small girl was trying to bowl a hoop, watched by an elderly nanny in white, with canvas shoes. Like mine, thought Angela. I wish I could get one like that for my children.

'The prospect from here is very good,' said the agent. He held a brown felt hat and she noticed that his collar was creased. 'For the rent – you'll hardly beat it.'

'Let me see,' she said, 'How many bedrooms?'

'Five on this floor, and two attics. Seven in all.'

It would suit her perfectly. Malcolm had said, 'Get a place by hook or by crook. I must start in five weeks.'

'How far is this from the new hospital?' she asked.

'About ten minutes' walk.'

Malcolm could do it comfortably.

They went into one of the back bedrooms. It would make an excellent nursery.

'I don't think you'll do better, madam,' the agent said. 'Unless you go out on the Tollhurst Estate. But there the rents are much higher.'

'And not so handy,' she added.

This was just the type of house she wanted: spacious rooms, an atmosphere of former elegance, and not too difficult to run. What prevented her from striking the bargain and taking possession?

Again she remembered Mrs Lumley, and her heart fell. If only she could be certain that Mrs Lumley had lived next door she'd take it on the spot. It was foolish to be so influenced by a ghost – especially when she could lay no charge against it.

'Yes. It's the sort of place I'm after,' she said, looking into the high-ceilinged, old-fashioned bathroom.

'It's all in good condition,' said the agent. 'Shall we see the attics?'

She jumped at the suggestion: it would give her time. They were nice long rooms, most suitable for the older boys. Keith could keep his books here, and David his wireless. She

wondered if Mrs Lumley's James had slept here. There she went again! I'm a fool, Angela said to herself, turning abruptly and going back down the narrow stairs. What's it got to do with me now – what happened years ago!

What had happened? She could not recall. Mrs Lumley had been a friend of her mother; she had been kind to Angela. Once her mother had said, 'You don't like Mrs Lumley, do you?' but Angela had risen hotly and denied it.

If only I could remember something definite, she thought angrily. They were now going downstairs into the hall. 'You'll look at the kitchen?' said the agent, leading the way. It was dark out there, and the gas stove was out of date. I would have electric, she thought; and a fridge. Was this where Mrs Lumley had been permitted by her cook to bake the cakes that afternoon?

'Now the drawing-room,' said the agent. Her heart beat faster. Perhaps she would land the elusive memory at last. They looked in for a moment at the breakfast-room, but it was so sunny and blank and strange that it gave her nothing. She paused only to take stock of the hatch connecting with the kitchen, and two frayed electric wires in the ceiling.

When they entered the drawing-room she looked round greedily. It seemed to be the same room – but were not the back rooms in all these houses the same? She tried to recall the wallpaper but, of course, it would have been changed since then. There had been a sofa facing the fireplace, covered in Nile green silk, with rose-embroidered cushions. Her mother, in a black dress, had sat with her back to the window. There had been a remark about the light and women of forty,

and both had laughed. Mrs Lumley, pouring tea, had sat beside the white-enamelled bell-pull.

But Mrs Lumley was still indistinct. Angela was strung up with the effort of remembering. She wanted to bring her back and to ask, 'Why don't I like you? Why cannot I take your house?'

However, it may have been next door after all. She turned to the agent. 'I'd like to have a word with your Mr Morgan before deciding. I want to know who lived here.'

'Very well, madam. But would you care to see the garden before we leave?'

He unbolted the french windows and they went out onto an overgrown lawn. The house was less formal from this side; a wisteria as thick as her wrist had been trained about the windows. She looked above the low wall at the house next door: the windows were shut; in one room the curtains were orange. It didn't look like Mrs Lumley's house. She looked back at the wisteria.

'It's odd,' she said to the agent, who was attending respect-fully. 'I wish I could make up my mind whether I've been here before.'

'It's difficult when the houses are so nearly the same,' he replied.

She walked away down the weed-covered path beside the uncut grass. To her right lay what was once a deep herbaceous border, in which some Michaelmas daisies and a few self-sown evening primroses struggled against the weeds. And now it began to come back to her: she had once been in this garden. Mrs Lumley was, trowel in hand, at work among the flowers.

She grew clearer: she was not tall; her skin was of an extra-ordinary velvety pallor and clearness. She smiled and her teeth were very white. 'You've brought something for me?' her voice was low and friendly. Angela handed her a note from her mother. Mrs Lumley laid down the trowel and read it. 'I'm so glad you can come to tea,' she said. Angela watched her. What a nice woman, she thought. 'Would you like to see my goldfish before you go?' 'Please,' Angela had replied. Mrs Lumley took her hand and led her down the path to the bottom of the garden. There was a pond there. Angela bent low over the water: beneath her own reflection, and Mrs Lumley's, some corpulent, golden-red fish moved slowly. 'They're lovely,' she said, excitedly. Mrs Lumley looked nearer, until her face was no more than a few inches away from Angela's. Then the child's attention was caught by something dark on Mrs Lumley's soft white face – on her chin, just below the jaw, was a large, brown mole. Angela stared with growing horror. It seemed not to belong to Mrs Lumley at all, but to be a vicious growth, of great evil, and more powerful than either Mrs Lumley or herself – almost like another person. She had gone cold all over, and silent.

Angela spoke to the agent. 'I think I'll just go to the end,' she said, 'There's something I want to see.'

Behind a box hedge lay the goldfish pond. There could be no doubt now. She looked back at the house: it awaited her decision.

'Yes. I will take it,' she called to the agent.

He smiled and took out his notebook. 'I don't think you'll regret it,' he answered, and began to write.

She went to the edge of the pond. It was practically empty: just a few dark leaves in the brackish rain-water a few inches from the bottom. She could no longer see, as on that day, the slow movements of the fish, backed by her own and Mrs Lumley's reflection. A lump came to her throat. 'Forgive me, Mrs Lumley,' she said.

IN THE BOATHOUSE

The Gasthaus stood on poor ground about fifty yards from the river bank, in a thin birch plantation. It was of pinewood weathered black as peat, with large built-out eaves; the sort of place you would expect to find in the south, in Bavaria – never so far north. During the monarchy it had been hunting lodge to the Schloss, but when the Baron fled the Gelders had been able to rent it for very little.

Fini, their daughter, enjoyed the air of desolation along the river bank and in the old walled-in garden of the Schloss where now the villagers and a few weekenders from Waldhausen grew their vegetables. When work at the hotel was over she escaped along the river path by the boathouse, which rot had made unsafe, and wandered about in the decaying forest behind the slate towers of the Baron's mansion. She spent hours there, as if in a dream, humming little tunes absently. She rarely met anyone unless it was the forester in his bottle-green uniform, or an old man with a clay-coloured sack routing tirelessly in the undergrowth. One day, in a remote clearing, she had come upon Abel collecting wood. He had been startled. 'I thought you were the forester,' he said; then decided to buy her silence with 'Would you like a drink?' and held up an

old army flask. The sun shining through the foliage made his face a yellow green. He was then fifteen.

That was two years ago. They had met each day since, unknown to her parents, in the old boathouse – until a few months ago when Abel – whose father, a boat-builder at Waldhausen, who had lately been in trouble with the political police – had become taken up with some work about which he refused to speak. There were days now when he did not come.

Fini set the wine glasses on the table in preparation for the anniversary dinner that evening and then went out into the hard sunlight. Where the river cut through the dry ground the brown reeds bent with the current, and beyond lay the shallow, ochre hills. The last four days had seemed to her to be without meaning – for Abel had been away. When last she had seen him, in the boathouse, he had been trembling, although the evening was not cold. As she watched him row down the quiet river and his white shirt had finally vanished in the blackness under a row of willows by the bank she had been stricken by cold herself – as if it were the last time they would meet.

He had said he would come tonight – to the boathouse at ten o'clock. But she could not forget her fear.

Frau Gelder came out to her. 'This is not the time for dreaming!' she said severely, folding her thick arms. Fini followed her indoors.

The local section of the National Socialists was holding the dinner. Each member had made a contribution: a fowl, pork, vegetables, and honey from the bee-keepers' club in the forest.

By midday the dining-room, still hung with the Baron's old trophies, was prepared, and Frau Gelder sent Fini to bring up beer from the cool cellars.

After the household's brief lunch, taken in the stacked kitchen, the baker from Waldhausen arrived with the bread, for which he had saved flour the whole year. He laid the basket down and stood with his belly thrust out. The sight of the food being prepared made his eyes light up. 'What's the good of belonging to the Party if you can't get a little extra now and then?' he said, smacking his lips. 'Look out for me tonight,' he said, with a heavy wink. 'You'll know me by my medals!'

'An old soldier, eh?' said Frau Gelder, nodding and smiling.

Fini went to the window and looked out. It was very hot and still; the birches looked like stage trees. Above the scrub in the direction of the river she saw the roof of the boathouse. She opened the window a little wider, but as she leaned on the sill her arms and shoulders ached with anxiety.

The baker was still with her mother at the door of the kitchen. 'And did I tell you that the Baron's son was my colonel? He used to come into the bakehouse and tell me I made splendid bread!'

After he had gone Frau Gelder mixed the stuffing for the fowl, and Fini and the two women who helped at the Gasthaus on special occasions prepared the vegetables. The afternoon passed slowly for Fini, who went often to the window.

At four o'clock Section Officer Gretsch arrived to see that all was in order for the feast at eight. Few would be late; all would be hungry. Frau Gelder took him through the kitchen and into the dining-room, where the photograph of the Leader

had been decorated with flowers. He expressed approval, saluted, and went. Frau Gelder returned in great haste to put the geese in the oven.

At half-past six Fini went to her room in the gable to put on her serving clothes. From here she could see the boathouse plainly, for it lay below her; shrouded by overgrown creeper and sheltering a few square yards of sluggish water left by the river it reflected the hot peace of the late afternoon; nothing stirred there. She went and lay for some moments on her high white bed.

At half-past seven the Nazis began to come by twos and threes along the forest path; against the pale greens and browns of the trees their mustard-coloured shirts and black breeches made them look as if they were made of cardboard. Frau Gelder was by now very excited and soon everyone, including Herr Gelder, in a striped waistcoat and bow tie, was at their posts. The two women helpers were in starched blue dresses, with their hair in Teuton plaits around their heads, and looked like twins. Fini hurriedly took her place at the serving-table in the dining-room, where her father was ladling out the soup.

For the next half hour she worked steadily, with little time to think of anything else, although whenever her eye caught sight of the window and the yellow light on the trees beyond she remembered. The men, elbow to elbow down the white dining-table, were noisy and full of jest, and when she looked into their cheerful faces she tried to smile for the sake of her parents. Once she was invited by the baker to taste his beer. She hurriedly brushed the foam with her lips, finding it

offensive. For some reason it made her think of Abel, and again she went down under her dread.

When the Nazis reached their cigars the room was thick with steam and smoke, and everyone was perspiring freely. To Fini the scene was remote, as if seen through cellophane. Her eyes sought the Bavarian cuckoo clock above the fireplace: the white hands on the brown face pointed at twenty-five minutes to ten. Those next twenty minutes went so slowly for Fini that she felt she would go mad. She stood with her back to the serving-table, screwing up her handkerchief, while a new member extolled the Storm Troops in a long, eager speech.

At five to ten she slipped into the kitchen and laid her apron on a chair. Her mother was giving Herr Gelder a scolding for upsetting so much of the beer in his haste to serve the diners. Unobserved Fini stepped outside. After the noise and heat of the house the twilight was sweet and cool. From among the trees near the Schloss could be heard the allotment-holders shouting to one another in the walled-in garden.

She set off at a run and by the time she reached the boat-house she was stumbling and panting. The door was covered with creeper, but not locked – Abel had prised it two years before – and pushing through the tall weeds she put her shoulder against it. Not daring to think what lay on the other side, she gave it a shove. It stuck. She pushed again, until she got her head and shoulders through.

'Abel,' she called in a whisper.

But all that lay on the water was the shaft of light which came through the door behind her, broken by her shadow.

Then it occurred to her that he was there, behind the door but had mistaken her for a stranger and had hidden. She gave their whistle – one, two, three: a short, a long, a short; but it was followed by silence. The water lapped the landing-stage softly, and beyond, under the drooping trees, lay the empty river.

She did not know what to do. She still felt he was close at hand and would presently appear. But although she repeated their whistle many times she received no answer.

About twenty minutes later she returned to the hotel, white and cold. The Nazis were still making speeches. The baker was interlarding his with stories of the Great War. Frau Gelder admonished her for being out so long, failing to see how pale she was.

Fini took up a cloth and began to wipe some beer mugs.

Through the open kitchen door the sky was still alight, but below, where the frail birches closed in around the Gasthaus it was now too dark to see anything. A little later a young moon rose behind the Schloss.

At eleven o'clock she went again to the boathouse. This time she was weeping. She called his name outside the door – but he did not answer. She slid to the dank ground and rested her sobbing head on the blistered paintwork of the door.

Three-quarters of an hour later she dragged herself back to the Gasthaus. The moonlight was as clear as a tumbler of spring water and the birches glittered like Christmas trees. From the lighted windows of the dining-room came the shouts of soldiers' songs – the Nazis were happy. Her father met

her at the kitchen door, too triumphant to notice the signs of weeping on her face: the evening had been a success. Even Frau Gelder, making a meal from the strands of flesh on the few remaining goose-bones, was pleased: her cooking and management had been praised by the Gauleiter.

A little after midnight the merry-makers began to go home. From her bedroom Fini heard their voices growing fainter through the woods. Finally all that was left was a murmur below her window – two Storm Troopers talking earnestly with her father. Soon they clicked their heels, called out 'Heil Hitler' with warm friendliness and went off with their boots ringing on the dry ground. The doors and windows were shuttered and bolted. She heard her mother ask 'Where's Fini?' 'Gone to bed,' came the reply, from one of the helpers. 'I expect she's tired – after such a busy day,' said Frau Gelder, in a kindly tone. They all came to bed and except for a drone of comfortable voices in her parents' room, which lasted about a quarter of an hour, the house was silent.

Fini lay and wept among damp and creased bedclothes. She did not know how to get through the night, and her despair deepened when she thought of wandering in the forest, but without Abel. However, so deep was the quiet in the Gasthaus that, without expecting it, she fell suddenly asleep.

About two o'clock she awoke, surprised to find herself still dressed. She sat up and looked round the room; the furniture stared back at her. Then, from the river, she heard Abel's whistle.

For a moment she was disbelieving, but again it came – clear and sharp. She scrambled to the floor and went to the

window. Below, the world was so still, yet so wide-awake. Cupping her hands round her mouth she whistled back.

Then she ran as silently as possible down the stairs, unbolted the kitchen door, and sped along the river path. The whistle could be heard again. Don't, she panted. Someone might hear. She pushed through the boathouse door into the blackness. This time she knew he was there.

'Abel,' she called, and a light sprang up. He was holding a match. She saw his yellow canoe pointing towards her on the black water and Abel within it, his face dark-eyed and white. As if in a dream she saw on the white shirt at his shoulder a bloodstain like a great dark rose.

'Oh!' she gasped, staring.

'Get in. Quickly,' he said, turning the match upside down. His voice was weak.

She ran along the landing-stage and climbed into the boat. It rocked as she settled herself near him and put her arms round his thin young shoulders. He was so frail, by contrast with the well-fed Nazis who had gone stamping home through the woods, and it seemed to her then that the thread of his life was like gossamer. Tense with pain he dropped his head against her shoulder. She took his wrist and drew his arm round her body.

Later, the river flow sucked the canoe from the boathouse and, in the moonlight, drifted it downstream to Waldhausen. Every now and then Fini kept it on its course by using the paddle with her free hand.

With his head on her shoulder, Abel slept deeply.

HALFWAY DOWN THE CLIFF

Since it was getting on for ten o'clock and his back ached, Percy laid his scythe down near the handkerchief containing his lunch and took a turn to the edge of the cliff. The weather was flawless: against the full blue of the sky where, for the moment, not a cloud strayed, the cliff was white as the ruffle on a ham bone, and below, the sea had pigment enough to be used as paint.

From this angle Percy was always fascinated by the light-house which lay under the steep cliffs like a nipple in the water. Today the rocks were visible: bottle-green and shiny as glass between the doe-like swirls of the sea. It seemed that you could just reach out your arm and touch the top of the lighthouse – although this was a delusion. (To get the truth of the situation it would be best to stand at the door of the lighthouse and to look up the three hundred feet of cliff to the straw-hatted speck above the tufted ridge which was Percy's head.)

It was at this point that he saw the child. He blinked and, drawing himself nearer the edge, pushed aside the curtain of grass. Far below him, against a moving background of rippling water, he saw the ledge – jutting out about three feet

from the perpendicular of the cliff – and on it, lying on its back with its arms and legs stuck out, a small object in a lace frock with a large blue sash round its waist. He pushed his straw hat in bewilderment to the back of his head, and scratched his sparse damp hair. 'Looks like a little girl,' he said. At that moment a seagull hovered near the child with its pointed head to one side, and then flew on unconcerned.

Percy gulped. The grass was tickling his chest through his moist shirt. He slid back from the edge of the cliff and sat up. The serenity of the day was broken. To action, said a voice in his head. He got stiffly to his feet and looked round for someone, but there was no one to be seen. Down the valley gleamed the unheeding, incurious faces of the two coastguards' cottages, tacked on to each other like Siamese twins, behind a pair of spruce gardens studded with cabbages. He went off down the hill, in his hurry slipping every now and then on the shining grass. Larks now rose at his approach and remained, immeasurably high up, straining their tiny lungs.

Mrs Welter had seen him coming. She came to the door of No. 2 shading her eyes against the glare with her right hand. Round her large waist hung a spotless white apron. She was probably going to have another baby. Her present two were engaged in threading beads in the shady kitchen behind.

Percy looked round awkwardly: he had no wish to scare her just then.

'Oh – er – ah!' He peered past her. May and Topsy stared back at him. 'Your chicks safe, eh?'

A shadow of anxiety crossed her face. 'You can see 'em for yourself.'

He jerked his thumb toward the next cottage.

'Mrs Thomas's Maggie all right?'

'Gone into town with her mother an hour ago. And would you mind telling me why you're asking?'

He looked at his large hands, corned with harvesting. 'Well, Mrs Welter – not wantin' to scare you and so on – there's a wee mite lying on the ledge yonder.'

She clapped her hand to her mouth. 'You don't say!'

'But I do,' he said gravely, 'and I've come for Coastguard.'

Mrs Welter called into the back garden and Mr Welter appeared, his waistcoat and shirt cuffs undone and the newspaper loose in his hand. He was wearing lead-rimmed spectacles and was rather short-sighted (strange in a coastguard – but there it was).

'You wanted me?'

Percy gulped as he said it this time: 'There's a wee mite on the ledge.'

Mr Welter's jaw dropped. He stared at him. 'I'll bring my binoculars.'

'And don't forget the rope,' said Mrs Welter. 'I'll send May down for the Constable.' Since Mr Welter suffered on and off with rheumatism PC Kitto effected all cliff rescues.

'Bring a blanket and some splints, a flask o' brandy and some rope,' chanted Mr Welter, like one asleep.

'Off you go now,' said Mrs Welter to May, who objected to having her game interrupted. Topsy, the youngest, was on the verge of tears until she heard a child had gone over the cliff.

'Oo – where?' she asked.

'Usual place,' said her father, 'Suicide Leap.'

'I expect some heartless profligate threw the poor little thing over,' said Mrs Welter, relishing a certain amount of rage.

The men started off up the hill, laden with equipment.

'Can I go too?' asked Topsy. She was wearing a bright red dress and her hair was tied into two short, stiff pigtails.

'If you don't get in the way,' said her mother.

She rushed off ahead of them, picking daisies as she went, and chanting in a high, thin voice: 'They threw her down the cliff, they did. They did.'

Percy and Mr Welter made the best pace they could, though neither was young and the day was growing hotter. Several times Mr Welter paused to rub the sweat off his forehead, while Percy adjusted his straw hat. Finally they drew level with the top of the hill and found the sea, like a carpet, staring up at them.

'Phew, what a climb!' said Mr Welter. 'Now where is the child?'

He slumped down on his belly at the spot where most people went off and put his binoculars to his eyes. At first he had them the wrong way up and everything, including the ledge with the child on it, looked several miles away. He corrected them hurriedly, hoping that Percy had not seen, and said:

'Looks like a mite about four, don't it! Wonder how she got there – wearing a blue sash and all. I do believe her eyes are open,' he added with excitement. 'Perhaps she'll see me if I wave.' He put his arm over the cliff and wagged his hand. 'That'll keep her going until we come.'

He sat back. The great sky grew denser with blue. 'It's going to be *hot*,' he said, looking up.

Topsy had come near the edge of the cliff. 'May I look, Daddy?' she asked carefully.

'Yes. If you don't fall over.'

He gave her the binoculars and she edged forward on her tummy. Presently she gave a little gasp.

'The baby's moving, Daddy,' she said.

He craned over. Yes, perhaps one arm had moved nearer the edge.

'Thank goodness,' said Mr Welter, 'we're going to be in time.'

Percy now came and lay face downwards with them, staring down the cliff. On the weed-draped rocks moved a silent and almost invisible army of black-headed gulls. Topsy looked at the lighthouse: there were men in there who ate, slept and played cards like anyone else yet, for some reason known only to themselves, they decided to live alone in a concrete funnel in the sea. She couldn't understand it.

PC Kitto and May found them stretched out on the edge. He had left his bicycle at the foot of the hill and was perspiring heavily. May had presumably ridden along behind.

'This'll be the fourteenth time I've been down this ruddy cliff to fish someone up,' said PC Kitto. He was clearly out of humour. 'Why people want to do these things beats me. Why they can't live at home like anyone else . . .' He had already taken off his coat and was tying Mr Welter's rope into a fire-man's hitch. '*I* don't come out and throw myself over the cliffs for a pastime. Here, hold this. . . .' He handed May the rope

while he went to a post a little way off which his father had once driven into the ground when he was about to rescue someone. He pulled at it. 'Holding pretty firm!' he said.

He turned to Mr Welter. 'How're you, Dick?'

'Prime,' said Mr Welter, dusting his knees.

'And you, Percy?'

'Fine,' answered Percy, also getting up.

'That's good,' said PC Kitto, getting into the fireman's hitch, 'because you've got to hold me pretty steadily – I'm in a hurry.'

'Depend on us,' said Mr Welter solemnly. 'I remember when . . .'

'Then take hold of the rope,' said the Constable. He was not going to waste time. That afternoon he was to take Mrs Kitto into town for the first time for several years and nothing was going to prevent him if he could help it, or he'd never hear the end of it.

It was now ten to eleven. Topsy, strengthened by May, was beginning to wander off, collecting daisies for a chain about five feet long. They had often seen people brought up the cliff, and it had ceased to be exciting.

Percy drew the rope round the post while Mr Welter made sure that PC Kitto's brandy bottle and first-aid kit were attached firmly. They now worked with an air of business-like precision: they had often dragged back a mortal who had thought never to see the world again.

PC Kitto went to the edge and peered over.

'Ah, there she is – the poor wee thing. We shan't be long now.'

Without looking down again he turned his back on the sea and began to scale down the cliff as quickly as if he were on a ladder. Before long his shoulders and head had gone, followed by his hands. All that Percy and Mr Welter had left to look at was the smiling face of the sea which said, as far out as the horizon: 'I have never done any harm to anybody. Look how peaceful I am!'

May and Topsy came running back.

'Where's Mr Kitto?' asked Topsy.

'He's climbed down the cliff,' answered Percy.

'Oh, I thought he'd fallen over,' said Topsy.

The Constable had run into difficulties. His seat was caught up on a tuft of thrift and, leaning forward, he had a job to get clear of it. Looking down he could see, a long way off, the inert form of the child. At that moment a light wind lifted the hem of her little skirt. A lump rose in his throat. 'Who would have the heart to throw her down,' he thought, renewing his effort to get to her against the steady release of rope from above.

When he had gone a little farther he looked up. Topsy had her head over the edge, no doubt on instructions from behind, to see how he fared. 'Coo-ee,' she called, giving him an ingratiating smile in which two upper teeth were missing.

Then he went and tore his trousers on a juniper bush growing in a crack. It would spoil Mrs Kitto's frame of mind for the afternoon, he felt sure. 'One day,' he swore, 'when I'm not in a hurry, I'll make a special trip and finish that bush off.'

He was now approaching the ledge which interfered with so many suicides. He called out:

'Hold on, duckie! I'm coming.'

He did not look down for some time, for he had a difficult piece of cliff to negotiate. When he looked again he was not more than five feet off the ledge, and staring down at the child. He had expected her to be pallid and frail after the fall, but she surprised him by the pinkness of her cheeks – almost apple-red beside the white cliff – and the sauciness of her full mouth. She could see him: her eyes were wide against her spread-out black lashes.

In a few moments he was on the ledge, undoing his brandy flask. 'Pull her together,' he thought, dropping on to one knee.

Only then did PC Kitto realise what the astute reader may have already tumbled to: the child on the ledge was not human at all, but a large doll. Of life-size, beautifully dressed, with eyes that opened and shut (the fall had somehow caused them to remain open), real hair glued to a life-size cranium, and a label attached to its neck on which were written the words: *My name is Polly*.

'Well, I never!' said PC Kitto, scratching his head in vexation. At that moment a stone fell from above – Topsy, no doubt, treading perilously near the edge. He looked up. Behind her Percy's straw hat was outlined against the blue. 'It's a doll,' he shouted. Percy put his hand to his ear and inclined his head.

'It's a *doll*,' the Constable yelled again, but Percy shook his head as much as to say he could not hear.

And then, since time was pressing, PC Kitto tied the doll's hands together, threaded his head between her arms,

and slung her on to his back. He then commenced to reclimb the spotless face of the cliff which, in the midday glare, dazzled him a little. As he went, careful to put his toes in the right places, he felt the steady lift on the rope of Percy and Mr Welter.

Halfway up he rested for a little while and looked out to sea. The lighthouse seemed nearer than ever. At that moment one of the keepers came out, threw some slops onto the rocks, and went in again, without seeing him.

He went on. As he neared the top he heard the excited cries of May and Topsy, who were leaning over giving those behind them a running commentary of the climb. 'He's saved her,' Topsy kept saying, 'I can see 'er on 'is back. Ever so pleased she looks.'

He gave one last mighty pull and heaved himself on to the horizontal. He lay for a moment or two, flat out on the grass, breathing heavily.

At that moment Mrs Welter arrived on the scene with a hot-water bottle, a thermos of tea, and a little doll for the child to play with. The Constable looked at her sadly:

'It ain't no use, mum. This here's a doll.'

'A *what*?' said Mrs Welter, aghast.

Her husband had tumbled to it. 'A doll, Maudie.'

Percy examined it. 'Sure enough – a doll.'

Mrs Welter came forward to see. Her eyes widened.

'Why – it's Topsy's,' she said, stupefied. 'The one she got in the raffle.'

She looked round for Topsy, but that individual was not to be seen.

'Come along out,' she said softly, and they all looked to where her eye had caught up on a bit of red skirt behind Percy's hips.

A very subdued figure emerged, its eyes large and guilty, and a finger stuck in where the two teeth should have been.

Mrs Welter regarded her with a lifted eyebrow.

'You are silly,' she said, before turning back to get the lunch, 'you might have broken it.'

THE SPLASH

When we handed in to the Schwimmbad attendant the neat boxes containing our clothes and valuables, he chucked us both under the chin, and asked:

'English?'

Ursula, in a reed-green bathing-suit, went down the duck boarding, but, being of a polite nature, I stayed to oblige.

'Yes.'

'From London?'

'Not very far away.'

'You like our beautiful Germany?'

'We are enjoying our visit very much.'

'If you want anything, come to me.'

He waved his hand into a little dark room behind him, well furnished with towels, bathing-suits, and rope-soled slippers. He gave an inviting wink.

'If you find it too hot out there, for instance.'

'Thank you very much,' I said, beginning to retreat.

Ursula, too, had made a hit with a young man in a little slip whose chest was covered with blonde curls. I interrupted brutally by plonking myself down on the sunbathing board next to hers.

'Ah,' said the young man; 'two of you!'

Ursula was disposed to make this one over to me, too, for she lay back on her board and shut her eyes.

'Yes,' I answered kind-heartedly.

'You have been far?'

'Just into Austria. We're on our way back.'

'Bavaria is very beautiful?'

'Very beautiful.'

'I come from Stuttgart.'

'Oh!'

'I work in an aircraft factory. Very hard. Only one Sunday in four do we get off, and most evenings we do Storm Trooper drill. That is why I laze on my holiday.'

That accounted for a naive pinkness of nose and shoulders.

'Very sensible of you.'

He leaned forward.

'Will you allow me to photograph you?'

I gave a fleeting glance at Ursula's closed face, but, before I had answered, his camera – a magnificent Leica – had been whipped out and adjusted against a prominent blue eye.

I smiled, and Ursula's better nature triumphed long enough for her to raise her head a little – before she lay back and covered it with a handkerchief.

The Storm Trooper drew up another board and lay down beside us.

'Have you got a Youth Organisation in England?'

'We've got the Boy Scouts.'

'But they're international.'

'We started them, though.'

He considered a moment.

'But they're not what I mean. I mean an official organisation like the Hitler Youth.'

'No; we haven't.'

'I thought not.' He smiled knowingly. 'It's a good training for the young. They learn to obey.'

There was silence. Then he began again.

'You don't like Hitler; do you?'

This was tricky. My German wasn't good enough to enter into a political argument, and to get out again. Ursula – drat her! – was no help at all.

'It depends on what you mean,' I answered vaguely.

'I mean this: you resent our pulling ourselves together so that we are a great nation once more. You don't want us to have colonies. The Versailles Treaty –'

'Bother the Versailles Treaty,' came from under the handkerchief.

'Your friend spoke?'

'I expect it was in her sleep.'

'Well, as I said, the Versailles Treaty tried to keep us down. We were slaves. The Führer has made us strong again.'

In the triumphant silence which followed I heard the shouts of two children splashing each other in the shallow part of the lake.

'He has made us proud once more.' His chest swelled.

'Would you like a bun?' I interrupted nervously.

He tapped his rucksack. 'Thank you, but I have my own.'

'Then, if you don't mind, I'm going to eat,' I said.

Ursula awoke. In exchange for a tomato, he gave us some sausage flavoured with garlic. Afterwards he lay picking his teeth.

But he was not going to let us off.

'Why don't you like Hitler?'

'He's too noisy.'

'That's not a reason.'

'Well, we don't like his Race Theory.'

That did it.

'It's difficult for you to understand – not being German.' The garlic-flavoured sausage wafted across our nostrils. 'But we have here, in Germany, the finest race of all – the Nordic. You've only to study our types to be impressed: fair-haired, blue-eyed, splendid physique. But we have too many other types – Jews and others – who are polluting the race. We have to get back our purity by exterminating those who do not belong.'

At that moment a gentleman in a striped bathing- suit came on to the lawn. He was corpulent, pure white, and had a head like an egg.

'Would you call him a Nordic?' asked Ursula.

Our friend hesitated. 'It would be necessary to make a thorough examination of his ancestry before I could reply.'

It now began to grow so hot that I felt I was in an oven.

'Well, I'm going to sleep,' I announced with determination. I slept.

Hours later, it seemed, I awoke at the sound of voices. Everything was papery white, and I had a bit of a head. Our friend was asking:

'When are you two going to swim?'

Ursula turned drowsily. 'What time is it?'

'Nearly four o'clock. I'm going in.'

He stood up and, pushing his chest out, did a few solemn exercises.

'As Storm Troopers we learn muscle control. We're physically and mentally fit.'

He waited to see what we would do, but we were so slow getting ready that he gave us up and, striding with his arms folded across his chest to the end of the spring-board, he peered down into the water. Returning, he was careful not to catch anyone's eye, although a few heads scattered about the lawn watched him with interest. Suddenly he turned, stood on his toes, and after counting one, two, three, sprang forward down the coconut matting. A few birds rose from the water at the sight of him and made off into the woods on the far side of the lake. We held our breath as he bounced on the edge of the spring-board and rose into the air.

But he must have been a bit heavy, for instead of doing a nose-dive, like a swallow, he shot out horizontally and landed on the water with an awful smack.

'Oh, my God!' said Ursula.

THE PIRATE

The bevy of beauty (in which I found myself) was led by the Colonel's wife into the entrance hall. The dance was being held by the military in one of the stately homes of England. The oak panelling had been carefully screened by lengths of white beaver-boarding and the drawing-room, in which we foregathered after leaving our cloaks, had been denuded of its treasures and looked like a schoolroom.

The Colonel – who was mouse-like and thin, and therefore not like a colonel – did the honours by his subalterns. It fell to my lot to find myself with the pirate.

He had blue-black hair and close-set, fanatical brown eyes.

His handshake was crippling.

'Pleased to meet you' – there was a trace of an American accent. He looked at me ferociously. 'Before we go any further let me make myself plain: I've lived the best years of my life on the prairies of Arizona – where a man's a man – and I've no time for all this insincerity,' he swept his arm round the room, 'introducing and suchlike. Where I come from we just see a women we like and that's that.'

After this opening I recovered with:

'So you're a bit of a wild man!'

'Not wild – just basic.' He showed a row of magnificent teeth. 'What'll you drink – or are you going to let me choose?'

'A sherry,' I said hastily.

'A sherry it shall be.'

He was gone in a moment to the end of the room, where a group of khaki shoulders were bent over the bar. He was a head taller than the rest.

In double quick time he was back. Raising his glass he said:

'Here's to the prairie.'

There was a challenge in his eye.

'You're English, I suppose. I was born here – that's why I came over to join up – but gee! how I hate it. It's feudal. The peasants are afraid to move because of the high-ups. With me, now, it's different: I don't give a damn for a high-up and if you ask any peasant along these roads if they know me they'll say "Gee, Lan Probyn's a swell guy." I've only one code and that's the prairie code – man to man.'

He smiled down at me. This time I noticed a gold stopping on a back tooth.

'Or man to woman,' he said. 'The law of the prairie says: if a woman takes a man he's not afraid to stand by her. In this country' – his eye swept the khaki-clad figures dotted about the room – 'the men are cowards.'

He was now gesticulating with an empty whiskey glass.

'Cowards and fops – except the peasants.'

'I wish you wouldn't call them *peasants*,' I said crossly.

His anger went instantly.

'I like a woman who answers back. Shall we dance?'

He was a good dancer if he had not jerked his left arm so much.

'In Arizona we're not afraid to let ourselves go when we dance. Here –' He left it in the air. The others were blissfully unaware of his scorn.

When we returned to the drawing-room he fetched more drinks. 'Now I'll tell you a little tale,' he began, settling into the sofa. 'When I was a youngster my mother made me a shirt: the collar was too small. When I was old enough for my first evening dress shirt: the collar was too small. I always have to have my collars two sizes bigger. Now why?' His face spread with pride. 'Because my ancestors were pirates, and they swung by their necks in a noose.'

At this point I was introduced to a young lieutenant with a fluffy fair moustache. He asked me to dance. When we returned the pirate eyed us ferociously. The fluffy-moustached lieutenant melted away.

'This is for you,' said the pirate angrily, handing me a pale drink.

'In the prairie country a man makes short work of inter-lopers,' he said. 'He also tells a woman what he thinks without beating about the bush.'

I glanced round anxiously.

Looking me in the eye he went on, his voice growing lower:

'He's also not afraid to ask her a certain question even if he's only just met her.'

The Colonel extricated me. I danced once more with the fluffy moustache and twice with an elderly major. Not long

after midnight the Colonel's wife gathered her party together and we bade the others good night.

The pirate was now stretched out in a chair with a tumbler hanging upside down from his hand. He was well away. Contrary to all rules and regulations he had taken the stud out of his collar.

SUMMER WITH THE BARON

Their congratulations unnerved her finally. Elisabeth almost wished she had never painted the picture, or that the gallery had turned it down.

'It's quite a sensation,' said an enthusiastic young man in a cord jacket.

'For one so young,' added someone with a red beard.

The Baron, standing a little way off, noticed her dull red flush and the agonised droop of her shoulders. The child was desperately put out. He went over and stood by her. Feeling his protective presence she slowly looked up into his round, peach-like face and smiling grey eyes.

'Pull yourself together,' he whispered. She seemed very nearly in tears.

She looked down his corpulent, middle-aged body to his square-toed shoes. She nodded.

'I want to make you an offer,' he said in an undertone. 'Will you paint a portrait of my niece?'

'I have had so little experience,' she answered faintly.

'Here is your opportunity then.' His smile broadened and sweetened. 'But I am afraid you will have to come to Germany – my niece is a cripple.'

Two months later, at the beginning of summer, she went.

Driving in the airy *Reichpost* she kept her shy gaze glued to the fields where the peasants were bringing in the first crop of hay. A middle-aged man, seated beside his expansive wife, observed her unpretentious English profile, her flaky hair combed off a narrow, high forehead, her brown brogues and woollen stockings; and beside her, the box of paints and the easel strapped together. 'She has come to paint our beautiful mountains,' he said proudly.

In her own mind beat the words of Aunt Judith: 'How kind of the Baron to give you a chance!'

The Baron's car was drawn up where the bus stopped. Shyly she let the thick-set chauffeur take her luggage and drive her to the Schloss.

As they turned at the top of the hill and the stone porch and high windows of the house came to view her courage failed her. She would have liked to turn and go. But a middle-aged and friendly woman had appeared at the door.

'The Herr Baron is in the smoking-room with Fräulein Tilda. I am instructed to take you there as soon as you have been to your room.'

The Baron greeted her warmly and led her across the room. 'Tilda, my dear. Here is your artist-companion for the summer.'

The Baron's niece was thin and undergrown. Partial paralysis had struck her early. Seated in a high chair by the window she watched Elisabeth intently.

Elisabeth took her small, limp hand, and then sat awkwardly in the chair the Baron placed for her. Tilda began to ask her questions about her journey.

The Baron felt that his instinct had been right. The girl was the right age for Tilda: about nineteen to Tilda's sixteen. It would bring something to Tilda's constricted life to learn about pictures and picture-making. As for the girl herself – the Baron smiled sympathetically as she tried with her smattering of German to hold a conversation with Tilda – she was a charming young woman, quite unsure of herself and her power over paint or people, too shy and young for her age, but touchingly sincere and serious. Altogether, he thought – supplying a word to aid the conversation – the visit should do both of them a great deal of good.

The Schloss was built above a lake and four great hills. From the top room, which had been converted into a studio, artist and sitter could look onto a velvet canopy of trees which stretched from side to side and, below, the row of pinewood bathing huts strung along the edge of the lake. They could watch the pinhead swimmers sliding out into mid-lake, and the minute silvery splash which followed a dive. When the sun swung over behind the first hill the water turned dark peacock blue and looked ice-cold but the bathing huts remained a warm umber and the bodies of the bathers a pinkish-brown. It was like looking down at the stage from the back row of the gallery.

'Uncle will take us there, one day,' said Tilda, during a rest. 'You mustn't work all the time.'

The two girls had quickly come to like each other. They stayed for hours in the studio, scarcely speaking, while Elisabeth made pencil studies of the crippled girl.

At eleven each morning the Baron came to take refreshment

with them. He would put his arm under Tilda's shoulders and support her to the window, or round the room. She could walk only with great difficulty, relying on two heavy black crutches.

'You must take Elisabeth to the lake, Uncle,' she said. 'Before it becomes too crowded.'

He turned to Elisabeth. She raised her eyes, caught his glance for a fraction of a moment and looked away like an animal startled, by a pool.

'Would you like to go?'

'When I have begun the portrait I should very much like to,' she answered formally.

Soon after he left they were back at work. Presently the silence in the airy room (the windows were wide) was broken by the cripple's sharp, almost gay voice.

'Do you like my uncle?'

For a moment Elisabeth was too absorbed to understand.

'I – I – Why, yes. Very much.'

Tilda was satisfied. Her thoughts flowed on. Presently she said:

'He's been so good to me. My mother was his sister. She died when I was born.'

Elisabeth looked up at the childish, sallow face. It had moved from position and was staring at the hills. Something helpless about the small curved mouth and waxlike cheeks affected her sharply.

'My uncle has always been so good to me,' came the soft voice. The child had forgotten Elisabeth was there.

The words brought the presence of the Baron into the room. In the cushion on the window-seat lay the imprint of

his knee; faintly she could detect what remained of his cigar-smoke.

Quietly she put down her pencils. Yes, the Baron was wonderfully good.

Two days later he took them to the lake. Elisabeth sat with Tilda in the back of the car while the Baron sat next to the chauffeur. They picnicked on the far side of the lake where the Baron had a six-roomed house with a wide gable, built of pinewood. In a shadowy boathouse which smelt of the turgid lake water, two skiffs were moored, while on the bank grew a profusion of silver birches.

The Baron and the chauffeur brought rugs and chairs from the house and arranged them on the soft ground. This side of the lake was in deep shadow. Across the water came the laughs and shouts of the people at the bathing station. Here and there in the yellow light lay the inert forms of sunbathers.

'We ought to go out in a boat,' said Tilda. 'It's dark here.'

The chauffeur, in his green uniform, was laying out the picnic basket. He did not look up: Fräulein Tilda could never go in a boat.

'I wish,' said the Baron, 'I had kept the other side of the lake.'

Elisabeth was lying on her elbow on the rug. The ground was still faintly warm from the early morning sun. Her fingers rummaged in the soft loam. She felt at peace, as if the tightly wound mainspring of her life had slackened. She turned her head back and looked at the Baron sitting upright in a canvas chair, his knees apart and his hands clasped across his waist-coat, like a small, active Buddha. He was watching Tilda's

delight at a butterfly which seemed about to fly towards them only to sheer electrically off again. Behind his round, close-cropped head stood the pinewood house. In the crook of the gable was a tiny window. The chauffeur had opened it to let in the air.

What a lovely house, thought Elisabeth, seeing it not in masses of colour or tone, but as a house where people could live and be happy.

Now the Baron was watching her. Nervously she shifted her gaze to the bathing station on the far edge of the lake, a noisy refuge from the intimacy of the little party under the birches and the pines.

The Baron had noticed. How shy the young thing is, he thought. We must try this summer to ease it away.

But he said nothing.

They went often to the lakeside. After lunch the crippled girl would lie back against her pile of cushions and read a novel, or sleep.

At first the Baron went alone for a walk in the woods while Elisabeth bathed in the lake, but later he suggested that she should go with him. Shyly she accepted and they went together through the deep woods which covered the mountainside. They spoke very little and climbed slowly, for the Baron was inclined to be short of breath.

At first she answered every word he addressed to her and was careful not to hurry or hinder him, but gradually she felt more at ease. One day they went over the mountain and sat in the sunshine outside a forester's log house, drinking some

white wine. The hills reached away before them like cardboard layers as the valleys began to fill with mist.

Again the sensation of peace came over her. She looked at the Baron. His white hand was round the bottom of his glass. He had said nothing for some time and seemed lost in thought. Elisabeth wanted to put out her hand and touch his arm. There was something she wanted to say to him, but she could not think of what it was.

After dinner that evening the Baron went to the window and stood for some minutes staring at the lake, which was now shadowy and deserted. He still wore the grey coat with the green collar he had worn on the mountain. Elisabeth noticed that his shoulders sagged a little. Suddenly he turned round.

'Tilda – Fräulein Elisabeth – I must leave you for a day or two. A telegram has come this evening,' he turned to Tilda particularly, 'from Uncle Basil. You must take care of each other until I return.'

When Elisabeth went to her room she felt startled and disappointed. As she brushed her hair her heart was heavy. The excursions to the lake would be meaningless if the Baron were not with them.

Next morning he went. At eleven o'clock their refreshment was brought to them by a rosy-cheeked maid. She laid it on a table by the window.

'Only two glasses today,' she said brightly.

The remark cast a gloom on them both. Elisabeth laid down her brushes and went to sit near Tilda, on the window-seat.

'I hope Uncle won't stay away too long,' said the child. 'Sometimes Uncle Basil keeps him for weeks.'

Listlessly Elisabeth looked out of the window: the mountains seemed forbidding, the lake deserted.

'I, too, hope he comes back soon,' she said slowly.

The Baron was away for three weeks. He arrived one evening, pale and tired out. As they sat with him by the window, and he smoked his cigar, the two girls said very little.

Next morning he came to see the portrait: it was finished. Arranging it in a cool, soft light, he observed it carefully, with his hands clasped behind his back. For some time he said nothing while Elisabeth silently and nervously packed away her brushes. Presently she heard his voice:

'Yes. It will do. I am well satisfied.'

He did not turn round.

She looked up through a streak of hair. Her face shone. But almost at once her happiness was crushed. Now that the portrait was finished she would have to return to England. She looked dejectedly at her handful of brushes until he turned.

He looked at her pityingly. Still she was so terrified. He took her warm, thin shoulders in his hands. Her mouth twitched.

'My dear,' he said, 'stay with us until the end of the summer. Tilda will enjoy having you.'

She looked at him through glistening tears.

'Thank you,' she said, almost inaudibly. 'Oh, thank you, Herr Baron.'

She stayed with them until the end of September, and then Aunt Judith wrote: 'Elisabeth dear, you really must come home.

I am beginning to feel very lonely without you and I am sure the portrait of the Baron's niece is finished by now. It couldn't take *all* that time to do.'

The letter arrived at breakfast but she could not bring herself to tell Tilda or the Baron just then. Down by the lake that morning (it was growing cold now and it would be one of their last visits) the thought of leaving them lay heavily on her spirit. More than ever the lake water seemed to have little buoyancy and she had to swim hard in order to keep afloat. When she climbed the wooden steps on to the bank she was breathing fast.

The Baron was reading a magazine. Tilda, against her pile of cushions, watched her come up the path.

'Elisabeth,' her voice was startled, 'you're cold. Your teeth are chattering.'

I must tell them, thought Elisabeth. She felt like lead.

'Tilda' – her wild glance included the Baron – 'I've got to go.'

The Baron looked up. Her shadowy, softly moulded face was turned away from them. He smiled so gently that it was barely noticeable.

Four days later they drove with her to the nearby railway station. From there she took a train to Munich. The thunderous, crowded city station where she had to wait an hour and a half was utterly different from the Schloss, folded in by the quiet hills, where the Baron and Tilda were at this moment continuing their peaceful lives.

She could not forget the last moments she had spent with them. The car with the hood back was drawn up on the road,

parallel with the train. The Baron was bolt upright beside the chauffeur; Tilda was propped up in the back, her sticks fixed beside her. Now and then they said something amongst themselves and then they turned to her where she stood on the steps of the carriage and smiled, or called something out. She wanted to climb down and run back to them and stay for ever in the security of the Baron's household. But presently the train drew out. The last she saw of them were their fluttering white handkerchiefs and a dazzle of glass and chromium as the car caught the sunlight on a bend.

Three hours later she reached Munich. She found herself a place in the express (it was almost full) and left her paints and easel on the seat. It was late afternoon and the platform was crowded. She bought a packet of chocolate and ate most of it at once, feeling dismal and alone.

A quarter of an hour before the train left she went to her compartment and sat down. Presently the other passengers came in. Among them was a tall young man in a tweed jacket and grey flannel trousers. He slung a tightly packed rucksack on to the rack and sat down opposite Elisabeth. She knew by his air of fresh health and self-confident untidiness that he was an Englishman just finishing a holiday. Not long after the train started he brought out a rye-bread sandwich from a packet and munched it slowly with strong white teeth.

As night fell, Elisabeth went into the corridor, where other people already stood watching the dim line of mountains to the south where, here and there, a peak still shone in the glow of the vanished sun. The train was now travelling very fast and the air which blew into the corridor was growing

colder. She wondered if she would ever see the Baron and Tilda again.

She felt a movement beside her and drew back. The Englishman had joined her at the window. Smart gusts of wind blew a lock of hair across his forehead. He smiled down at her.

'Don't move, please. There's room for two.' He ducked down to see out. 'This is the best time of the day.'

They stood shoulder to shoulder as the long white fields and knots of farms and cottages passed away behind them.

When it was too dark to see anything more, and the noise of the train had shut out what was left of the world, he looked down at her:

'I expect you're feeling a bit cold, aren't you?'

She had turned up the collar of her jacket.

'How about coming along to the refreshment car and we'll have a warm up?'

She looked at his eager fair face which waited confidently for her answer. She hesitated for a split second and then she answered with a new kind of recklessness:

'I'd love to.'

'Right you are. Follow me.'

He turned and she went down the corridor behind him, threading her way between the people and the luggage, careful not to lose sight of his broad brown back.

At the door of the refreshment car the young man turned:

'Ah, there you are. I was afraid you'd got lost.'

She preceded him into the brightly lighted car. One or two people looked at them.

'How about this?' he said, directing her to a table with a large, friendly hand.

Seated opposite the young man in the swaying, clattering train, hemmed in by the hum of talk and the hurrying attendants, she felt a deep flow of happiness. Her limbs became heavy and relaxed.

Just then she caught his eye and smiled.

THE VISITATION

There are places on the South Downs where the walker suddenly comes upon a cottage, or pair of cottages, puritanical in shape and usually built of flint and brick, with a slate roof – the 'council house' of seventy years ago. The bleakness of the location is always startling: either it is built in a fold of the hills where on warm days there is little air, or else it battles against the four winds on the plateau of a remote hill. Sometimes there is a garden in which a few cabbages grow dismally, hemmed in by a falling wall, or a row of flints: all that testifies to a lost struggle against the wild soil.

More often than not such cottages are deserted – their spiritless square windows wiped out by slabs of boarding – but occasionally an undergarment swinging on a wire line, or a child's toy beside the front door, make a murmur of life in the barrenness of the countryside. It is often a shepherd and his wife who live there, and sometimes a tinker and his brats, tucked up for the winter on very little rent – their old lorry, used for trading rabbits into town, parked on the windy side, lashed dull and rusty by the incessant squalls.

Lethbury, the shepherd, lived in a house such as this. It was semi-detached and the one next to it had been empty for

years. His sheep grazed along the ridge and, in wild weather, in the sheltered hollows which overlooked the weald. His eldest child, Nan, was fifteen; the next two, both girls, went to school three miles away, taking their food with them; the youngest, a boy, had not long been born.

Mrs Lethbury, who had been the daughter of a sweep in town, had at first found the hill too solitary. The few wild flowers which she saw from her door were not enough to keep her company, and it was not until the arrival of her family that she could settle down.

In the autumn of 1940 Nan started work in the nearby town. When she returned at eight o'clock her father, a small quiet man, was generally at home – in warm weather digging in his patch of garden, or hugging the fire with his shirt undone if it were cold or damp. On Sunday evenings he would slip down the hill to the village and drink with the other men. But in lambing time he was like a woman: confident and tender. At such periods he spoke hardly at all, and seemed to live apart.

The cottage faced east and there were no windows either to north or south, although these aspects commanded the view. To the north lay the weald, a perpetual pattern of richness, and to the south ran the long valley that finished abruptly in the chalk edge against the sea. Into the flat ocean pushed the crooked arm of the jetty. On summer evenings the water glistened like mother-of-pearl, and before the war the cross-channel steamers came like cardboard boats over the faint horizon.

From here the air-raid siren starting up in the harbour

town below, or from the one or two small towns in the weald, sounded gnat-like and unimportant. To Lethbury, it carried little danger. He sat all May with his sheep, waiting for the planes to go, safe in the wildness of the hill. But to his wife the warning was more impersonal: the lone house seemed to be a target for the bombers. She wrapped the baby up and told the children to come indoors, or worried over them if they were at school. It was a long while before she could be persuaded out at night, when the raiders crept in, high up, on their way to London, to see the roads of frozen gas left against the stars.

Then one evening in September the hill itself was visited. At nine o'clock they had their supper; the youngest children were in bed and Nan had just come home. When he had finished his meal Lethbury put down the evening paper and fitted the squares of plywood into the window sockets. Mrs Lethbury lighted the lamp.

Twenty minutes later the thin call of the siren came from the harbour and in a little while the Lethburys, on their lonely hill, heard the approaching hum of the first raider. It was followed by a second, and a third, and a fourth.

With stiff arms Mrs Lethbury began the washing-up, while her husband stoked the fire. Then she came and sat in the rocking chair with her knitting in her hands. Nan stared with fixed eyes at a picture in a magazine which she had spread out on the table. They were all listening to the bombers overhead.

At ten o'clock the even rhythm was broken by a new beat. They heard a raider flying lower – it seemed to circle over

them several times – followed by a curious rustle, like a great satin curtain being drawn across the sky; and the windows and doors of the cottage rattled as the hill shook.

Lethbury got to his feet. His narrow face was pinched with anxiety. His wife said nothing, but laid her knitting on the table. Her face was bloodless.

'Screen that lamp,' he said nervously. Nan turned it down. He went to the door and opened it.

The pantomime green glare outside almost stunned him.

'What the 'ell –' he began.

The bright landscape, clear as by day, gleamed eerily against the blue-black screen of the sky. He could pick out the slate roofs of the town below and even the yellow stonework of the jetty. Here and there, scattered in the now burning heather, lay hundreds of bright centres of fire.

'Min,' he called back to his wife, 'get the children down.'

She came to life at once and went upstairs. Nan followed her father outside. The cottage was revealed with uncanny clearness. A cloud of green smoke had now begun to hover over the valley.

'What is it, Dad?' she whispered.

'Incendiaries,' Lethbury answered shortly. He looked about him. Thank God his sheep were on the other side of the hill.

He turned to Nan. 'I must git down into Hollow Bottom. You can look after Mum, can't you?'

She nodded, her round face clear and bright in the glare. He went in and got his cap, and then he went round to the kennel and untied the dogs. They yelped up at him with joy

and fear as he went off down the hill. Mrs Lethbury called after him:

'Where'll you be?'

'Near the 'ut,' he called back. His voice was expressionless – he had closed himself up.

She knew it was no use saying anything more: she had long ago conquered the jealousy she once had felt when her husband chose his sheep before his children.

The children were downstairs on the wooden stairs, wrapped up in their overcoats. They were still half asleep. She took the baby up and rocked him gently.

Nan went to the well and drew up bucket after bucket of water and filled the half-empty water-butts (it had been dry that summer) while the waves of aeroplanes continued to pass overhead. When the well was nearly dry she let the lid drop.

By now the incendiaries were practically out – those left burning were no brighter than candles. Here and there where the heather smouldered a flame sprang to life for a moment, only to go out again. It was smoke now which filled the air.

She went indoors.

Fifteen minutes later the drone of the solitary raider returned. This time it was high explosives which fell along the hill. They could not tell where or how they fell, but sat crouching before the fire. The ground rumbled and rocked, while the house seemed as if it would collapse. Then came a storm of bomb splinters and clods of earth and flint on the roof, and the room was filled with powdered chalk as the door burst open.

They sat on in the cottage, the children pressed close to their mother, until the sound of the planes went to nothing, and the sky was empty. In a surprisingly short while the air had cleared and the stars once more queened it in the night.

In the cottage a coating of dust made everything white. Nan lit the lamp and put the kettle on to make some tea.

At half-past one she took a flask down to her father in the Bottom. The dogs barked in alarm as she made her way among the gleaming white bomb craters which now pock-marked the hill.

Her father was sitting by the grey, almost invisible sheep.

He stood up to stretch while, in silence, she poured out his drink.

"Tis good,' he said contentedly, drinking the strong black tea. 'It warms 'm up inside!'

If you have enjoyed this Persephone book why not telephone or write to us for a free copy of the *Persephone Catalogue* and the current *Persephone Biannually*? All Persephone books ordered from us cost £12 or three for £30 plus £2 postage per book.

PERSEPHONE BOOKS LTD
59 Lamb's Conduit Street
London WC1N 3NB

Telephone: 020 7242 9292
sales@persephonebooks.co.uk
www.persephonebooks.co.uk